"I had every intention of honoring our agreement."

Cara's tone was pleading. "And I've tried."

"I know that," Nick allowed.

She would have given a great deal at that moment to see into his mind, his heart. Surely his male pride had been badly wounded.

"Then you'll let me leave?" She tried to keep the eagerness out of her voice.

"No," he said flatly. "I told you I wanted a wife, and that I want you. Besides—" He broke off, frowning, as though he had said more than he had intended.

Besides what? He'd said last night that he would leave her alone until she came to him. Was he counting on her eventual surrender? It was what she had agreed to. But to go to him willingly....

ROSEMARY HAMMOND lives on the West Coast but has traveled extensively through the United States, Mexico and Canada with her husband. She loves to write and has been fascinated by the mechanics of fiction ever since her college days. She reads extensively, enjoying everything from Victorian novels to mysteries, spy stories and, of course, romances.

Books by Rosemary Hammond

HARLEQUIN PRESENTS
802—THE HABIT OF LOVING
859—MALIBU MUSIC

HARLEQUIN ROMANCE
2601—FULL CIRCLE
2655—TWO DOZEN RED ROSES
2674—THE SCENT OF HIBISCUS

ROSEMARY HAMMOND

loser take all

Harlequin Books

TORONTO • NEW YORK • LONDON
AMSTERDAM • PARIS • SYDNEY • HAMBURG
STOCKHOLM • ATHENS • TOKYO • MILAN

Harlequin Presents first edition July 1986
ISBN 0-373-10896-6

Original hardcover edition published in 1985
by Mills & Boon Limited

CHAPTER ONE

CARA stood at the kitchen stove, coffee pot in hand, frozen in place as she strained to hear the low muttered conversation between her father and brothers. Had she heard right? No, it wasn't possible. It must be a mistake. Slowly, she set the pot down on the burner, took out the frying pan from the drawer at the bottom of the stove and set it on another burner.

The four men were seated at the round breakfast table by the window talking in low tones, and Cara could catch only a word or an isolated phrase now and then. With their heads huddled together, they obviously didn't want her to hear. She was used to being ignored, but not deliberately shut out altogether.

She laid strips of bacon in the warm frying pan and listened carefully over the sounds of the bacon sizzling in the pan and the rain driving against the windowpanes. It was still dark out, not quite dawn. The boats had to be ready to leave at first light.

Impossible to believe, but it began to sound more and more as though her first shocked impression had been right. Somehow, her father had lost the two charter fishing boats that were the family's only source of income. But how could you 'lose' two forty-foot boats?

She knew better than to quiz them. Patrick would tell her later. Silently, she set the plates of bacon and eggs down on the table before them, filled their coffee cups and then went upstairs to check on her mother. She was still sleeping, Cara was thankful to see. She tucked the covers more securely around the wasted body and smoothed the hair back from a face lined and gaunt with the vestiges of the painful disease that was slowly killing her.

By the time Cara had made her own bed and gone back downstairs, the men had pulled on their boots and were shuffling out of the kitchen to get ready for the day's early morning charters.

'Patrick,' she called softly as they began to troop out the back door. He turned around to face her, then lowered his eyes at the enquiring look on her face. She walked slowly towards him. 'Patrick, what is it?'

He raised his eyes, then, the same clear piercing emerald green as her own, and she reached out a hand to him when she saw the hopeless look on his face. His shoulders were slumped forward in defeat.

'You heard?' he asked at last.

She shook her head. 'Not all of it. Tell me.'

He sighed. 'Dad lost the boats.'

'I gathered that much. But how?'

Patrick's mouth tightened into a thin line. 'In a poker game. Can you believe it?' He seemed close to tears. 'The old fool got drunk last night and lost our livelihood in a poker game.'

At twenty-five, Patrick was the youngest of the three O'Neal boys and the closest to Cara in age, just a year older. He was also the only one of the four men of the family who treated her as though she had some claim to adult human status. They looked alike, thought alike and had both inherited their mother's sensitivity. Cara longed now to reach out to him, to comfort him, but long years of habitual reserve stopped her.

'How could he?' she said bitterly. How typical of her father to think only of his own pleasure and totally ignore not just his sons' inheritance, but the needs of his sick wife.

Patrick shrugged. 'You know Dad. When he wants a thing, he just does it.'

'Who would do this to him?' she whispered.

'Nicholas Curzon,' Patrick said glumly.

Cara could only stare. 'Nicholas Curzon? But he's a professional gambler.'

At the sudden flare of anger in his sister's eyes, Patrick raised a hand. 'It wasn't his fault. Dad knows who he is, what he does. He was the one who insisted himself on betting the boats.' He laughed harshly. 'You know what he's like. He was going to show that city slicker just how clever a poor dumb Irish fisherman could be.'

Just then her father began shouting for Patrick from outside.

'You'd better go,' Cara murmured. 'We'll talk later.'

Patrick nodded, grabbed his heavy yellow slicker off the hook by the back door and was gone.

Cara stood at the kitchen window watching as the four men came around the side of the house and started walking down the road to the boat dock, just four blocks from the house. A pale grey dawn was breaking. It was still raining. Cara hugged her arms to her body with a little shiver of fear.

What in the world were they going to do? How would they live without the income from the charter service? How would her mother get the medical care she needed?

Nicholas Curzon! She could hardly believe her father would be so stupid as to play poker for such high stakes with a man who made his living out of gambling. He must have known he wouldn't have a chance! And how could Nicholas Curzon have taken advantage of him like that?

She shivered again and rubbed her hands over the goose bumps on her bare forearms. Just the thought of that tall, silent man was enough to make her shudder, much less the idea that the whole family was now in his debt.

He'd been coming every summer to the little village of Southport on the rugged Washington coast for something like ten years now. He knew quite well the precarious nature of the family business. He had been to the shabby weatherbeaten cottage many times, had seen how they lived, and most certainly knew of her mother's illness.

She thought of those watchful eyes of his, dark, sinister, almost dangerous. She always avoided him as much as she decently could and treated him with stiff politeness, as one of her father's best customers. He made her uncomfortable with his brooding gaze, and whenever it fell on her she had the disquieting feeling that somehow he could see into her most secret self.

By afternoon, she was so angry at both men that she felt faint with it. The only small ray of hope was that perhaps now Patrick could get away on his own, out from under his father's thumb. This thought made her feel a little better. Perhaps the three of them—she, Patrick and their mother—could leave the drab, isolated village on the ocean and build a new life together somewhere far away.

Even while she thought it, however, she knew it was hopeless. What could they do? How could they live? Even if she could get a bookkeeping or secretarial job, who would tend her mother? And all Patrick knew was fishing. It was only a wild daydream.

Today's charters were only one-day trips, so the four men were back at the cottage by seven o'clock. It was mid-September, and the light would be gone soon. Cara was in the kitchen preparing dinner when she heard them stamping their feet heavily on the back porch.

When her father came in, he called to her across the room on his way upstairs. 'We're having another for supper tonight. Lay on an extra place. And we'll eat in the dining room.'

She turned to face him, masking the anger and contempt she felt for him with her habitual calm exterior. 'There's only pot roast.'

'If it's good enough for us, it's good enough for him,' he muttered gruffly. He passed by her without a glance and began to clump up the stairs.

She and Patrick were alone in the kitchen now, and she gave him an enquiring look. Reading the question in her eyes, he nodded.

'Yes, it's Curzon. Dad invited him to dinner tonight. I think he has some crazy idea he can work out a deal with him. You know, keep the boats and pay him off a little at a time.'

Cara laughed humourlessly. 'It can't be done,' she said bleakly. 'I keep the books. I should know. We're operating on a shoestring as it is. Mother's medical expenses and keeping the boats in good repair take all our profits.'

'I guess he feels he has to try,' Patrick said wearily. 'You know, I almost feel sorry for him. He knows he was wrong. He's trying to do what he can to remedy the situation. It all depends on Curzon.'

Cara gave him a tight smile. 'Maybe I should put a dose of arsenic in his dinner.'

Patrick grinned. 'Good idea, except, knowing you, the first thing you'd do if you got caught would be to confess.'

'Cara,' her father bellowed from upstairs. 'Have I got a clean shirt?'

'Coming, Dad,' she called back. She rolled her eyes at Patrick and went up the stairs.

Nicholas Curzon appeared promptly at six o'clock. Cara had barely caught a glimpse of him before dinner as she laid the table and carried food into the dining room from the kitchen. The moment he came, her father had dismissed her brothers and the two men had sat in the living room, their heads close together, deep in quiet conversation. As she worked, she glanced in at them occasionally, wondering what kind of deal her father could possibly make with the tall, forbidding-looking man. He was deeply tanned, and even in the rough clothes that were customary wear in the fishing village, he had an air of slick, smooth sophistication. Her father would be no match for him.

At dinner, sitting across from him at the table, she could barely look at him without loathing. He spoke little. All his movements, as he ate, or drank the cheap wine, were controlled and economical. His expression was bland, the eyes so guarded that she couldn't make out their colour until, halfway through the meal, he turned his direct gaze on her for the first time and spoke to her.

'This is a fine meal, Miss O'Neal,' he said in his deep voice. 'Quite an improvement over the food at the motel.'

Cara shrugged and looked with barely concealed hostility into the hard grey eyes. 'It's only family fare, Mr Curzon,' she said at last in a flat unfriendly tone.

The silvery eyes flashed momentarily, then he smiled imperceptibly and the lids came down again as he turned to her father and they began to discuss the next day's fishing.

This is insane, she thought, as she silently finished her dinner. Here was her father calmly discussing the tides and last year's salmon catch with the man who was going to ruin him. She made up her mind to confront her father the moment Nicholas Curzon was out of the house. For her mother's sake, if not her own, she had to find out just where matters stood. Perhaps her father had convinced him to accept instalments on the gambling debt, but she couldn't see how they would manage to make even token payments.

As she moved about the room after dinner, clearing away the dishes, pouring out the coffee, she had the odd feeling that the man was watching her from those guarded grey eyes. It was hard to tell. There was a cool air of professionalism about him, as though he saw everything and gave away nothing. How could her silly father have been such a fool! It was so obvious what kind of man he was.

In his dark trousers and heavy black turtleneck sweater, he reminded her of a panther lying in ambush, ready to pounce on his unsuspecting prey and devour it.

She was in the kitchen running water into the sink when he appeared at the doorway and called her name. She turned off the water, dried her hands on a towel and slowly turned around.

'I'm sorry to interrupt,' he said in his low quiet voice. 'I'm leaving now and wanted to thank you for the dinner before I go.'

Their eyes met for a brief moment, and she almost thought she saw something like a plea in his expression, as though he were seeking her approval—or her forgiveness. No, she thought, that wasn't possible. A man like Nicholas Curzon would never ask, he'd only take. He wouldn't care about anyone's approval, he would do as he pleased. As for forgiveness, that was laughable.

She merely nodded at him then, and turned back to her dishwashing. Just go, she thought. His very presence in the house made her uncomfortable. Her life had been far from a bed of roses before his arrival into it, but now it was fast becoming intolerable. She *had* to have it out with her father. Tonight.

When she finished the dishes she turned out the light in the kitchen and went into the living room. The boys had apparently either gone out or gone up to bed, and her father was alone, seated at the old rolltop desk in the corner of the living room, staring down at the account books, his head in his hands.

'Dad,' she called softly. He turned his head and glared at her. She walked towards him. 'Dad, I want to know what's going on.'

'Never mind,' he said gruffly. 'It's not your affair.' He turned back to the books.

'It *is* my affair, Dad,' she said in a firmer tone. 'I keep the books, remember? I'm going to find out sooner or later.'

He looked at her again, anger written in the firm set of his jaw and hard blue eyes. He opened his mouth. Then, to her amazement, his face crumpled. 'Just let it be, Cara. It's my worry, not yours.'

'Maybe I can help,' she said more gently. 'Won't you tell me?'

Then, haltingly, without looking at her, the story came out. He had indeed lost the boats to Nicholas Curzon in a poker game. Now he was trying to negotiate with him to pay him the value of the boats in instalments. When he had finished the sorry tale, Cara sat down in the chair next to him and thought for a moment.

Then she said, 'Why pay him at all? What can he do? Sue you? I can't imagine any court in the country giving a rich gambler title to your boats, your family's livelihood, over a silly game.'

He only stared at her for a long moment. Then he shook his head. 'You don't understand. I've already given him my personal notes. Not only that, it's a matter of honour. I made the bet. I'm responsible.'

'Dad, that's crazy. He's a professional gambler. He probably cheated you.'

'No, Cara, he didn't cheat me. And he's not exactly a gambler. He owns a casino in Nevada, but he's not a professional. He won fair and square. It's a matter of honour,' he repeated firmly.

Honour! Clara thought bitterly. And they call women the weaker sex! What kind of honour was it for a man to calmly hand over everything he owned to another man over a game? She knew it was useless to argue with her father. His stubbornness was legend.

She rose from her chair. 'I have to go tend to Mother,' she said with a sigh.

He gave her a sharp look. 'Don't you go telling her about this,' he commanded sternly.

'Oh, Dad, she's bound to find out.'

He nodded. 'In time. But not yet. Not until I have Curzon's agreement.'

'That Judas!' she said bitterly. 'How can you trust anything he says?'

'Now, don't you go blaming him,' her father warned. 'He didn't cheat me. He didn't trick me. He didn't put a gun to my head and force me into that game. It wasn't even his idea. It was all my own doing.'

Nick came to dinner the next night, and the next. It was always the same. He and her father would talk business before dinner, and he left immediately after the meal. He always complimented Cara on the meal and thanked her politely before he left.

Although those brief exchanges were the only conversation they had, she was intensely aware that the piercing grey eyes continued to follow her every movement. It was as though he was silently appraising her, assessing her with his distant hidden gaze, and it was always a relief to her when he left.

She wondered what the reason was for this constant surveillance, and once or twice, when she

glanced at him, she saw something in his
expression that looked very much like appreciation,
almost desire. This astounded her, and she decided
later that she must be mistaken. She detested the
man, and although she observed strict courtesy to
him as a guest of her father, he couldn't possibly
mistake her feelings. Not by a word or a gesture
had she shown him anything but a frosty
politeness.

Besides, a man like Nicholas Curzon would
have no interest in her. She had spent virtually
every day of her life in Southport, with only a few
rare trips to Seattle to show her what city life was
all about, enough to tell her she didn't want it.
What she really wanted, she couldn't have.

On the night of his third visit to the house, when
she was getting ready for bed, she thought again
about those few looks he had given her. Surely she
was mistaken. He would have to be a remarkably
omnivorous and unselective predator for her to
arouse any desire in him, with the old shapeless
clothes she wore, the total lack of make-up and the
casual way she knotted her heavy black hair at the
back of her head.

Yes, she had to be wrong. She prayed she was
wrong. The mere thought of being the object of
Nicholas Curzon's desire was totally repellent to
her. All she wanted was for her father to reach
some kind of agreement with him about the boats
so that he would leave Southport and go back to
the hole he had crawled out of. It seemed hopeless,
but as she said her prayers that night, she
reminded herself wearily that nothing was truly
hopeless.

*   *   *

On the fourth night he came to dinner, Cara noticed a subtle change in the atmosphere. While she was preparing dinner she could hear voices raised in the living room, and during the meal there was a strained silence. This night no one even made a feeble attempt at polite conversation.

As usual, Cara sat eating quietly, not speaking, her eyes on her plate. In the awkward silence she was even more intensely aware of the tall dark man's gaze on her, and she was relieved when they had finished and she could get up and clear the table.

She had just finished the dishes when he appeared, as usual, in the doorway. She turned around when she heard him and waited for him to express his thanks for the meal, anxious to have him out of the house. Instead, however, he only stood there with one shoulder resting against the doorframe and watched her with those hooded, appraising eyes.

'Miss O'Neal—Cara,' he said slowly in a flat, expressionless tone.

'Miss O'Neal will do,' she said sharply.

His face hardened at that, the gaze narrowing, but then a flicker of a wry smile appeared on his thin mouth. He nodded. 'Very well. If you prefer. Will you come into the living room? I want to speak to you.'

She stared coolly at him. What did he want with her? Suddenly she remembered those brief looks he had given her, and a little shaft of apprehension pierced into her heart. He looked so tall, so threatening, so arrogant, standing there waiting for her. Even though his expression was courteous, his manner patient, the power he wielded over her whole family was frightening, and they were both aware of it.

She turned from him to hide the fear and slowly dried her hands. He must know she kept the accounts. He would naturally want a clearer picture of their financial situation. Well, he was in for a shock, she thought drily, if he expected to bleed them for any sizeable amount of money.

She turned back to him. The wild thought crossed her mind that maybe she could appeal to his better nature, at least try to make him see their predicament. 'Very well,' she said, and walked towards him.

He stepped aside to let her pass through the doorway, and when she reached the living room, she saw that it was empty. Apparently her father had given up. She walked over to the desk to get her books.

'Please,' she heard him say behind her. 'Sit down. Over here.'

She turned to see him gesturing towards the sofa. 'I'll just get my accounts . . .' she began, opening a drawer of the desk.

'No need,' he broke in. 'I've already seen them. Come and sit down. I just want to talk to you.'

Silently, she obeyed. She sat gingerly at one end of the sofa, as far from him as she could manage, and turned to him, waiting. He lowered his tall frame down at the other end and put one arm casually over the back of the couch. He didn't speak for a few moments, and when he did his voice was flat and matter-of-fact.

'You think of me as some kind of monster, don't you, Cara?'

It wasn't what she had expected at all, and she

gave him a sharp glance. He seemed to be totally
at ease, his long legs stretched out in front of him,
his expression bland and inscrutable. Cara looked
down at her hands, lying quietly in her lap.

'I don't know quite how to answer that, Mr
Curzon,' she said slowly at last. 'I don't really
know you. To be fair, I have to admit that it was
probably my father's own foolishness that landed
us in this mess, but I'm afraid you can't expect me
to have warm feelings about the person who took
advantage of that foolishness.' When he remained
silent, she looked over at him. 'What are you
going to do? If you've seen the books you surely
know we wouldn't be able to pay off the value of
the boats in a hundred years.'

'I'm aware of that.'

'Well, then, your only alternative is to sell them,
isn't it?' Although she kept her voice steady,
determined not to beg or grovel, the note of
contempt in it was quite apparent. 'Do you need
the money from them as badly as we do?'

'They are my boats now,' he reminded her
softly. He straightened up and leaned slightly
towards her over the empty space in the middle of
the sofa. 'But that isn't what I wanted to talk to
you about.'

'I can't imagine that you and I could possibly
have anything to say to each other, Mr Curzon,'
she said stiffly. She gazed directly at him. 'You
may have a legitimate claim on those boats. I
don't know. I doubt it, but my father seems to
think you do. That makes you the enemy, and no
amount of conversation can change that fact.' She
started to rise to her feet. 'Now, if you'll excuse
me . . .'

'Sit down!' he barked.

She was standing now, and gazed down at him, wide-eyed. 'You have no right . . .'

'I said sit down, damn it,' he repeated. 'I have every right. Do you want to help your father keep his boats or not?' He glared up at her.

Slowly she sank back down on the sofa. It was the first sign she'd seen in him of any emotion whatsoever, and she didn't know quite how to handle it. As was her habit, however, she remained quite still, her hands folded in her lap, watching him. After all, he held all the cards. She'd better listen to what he had to say.

'That's better,' he said in a kinder tone. Suddenly he smiled. 'You don't give anything away, do you, Cara? I don't think I've ever met a woman who called less attention to herself. You'd make a very good poker player.'

'That's not one of my ambitions,' she rejoined curtly. His careful scrutiny was beginning to make her nervous, and she had to summon forth all her power of will not to show it.

'What are your ambitions?' he asked.

She looked at him. What did he care? 'If I had any, I'm sure you wouldn't find them at all interesting.'

'Oh, but you're wrong.' He leaned closer towards her. 'Tell me about yourself. I've been coming up here to the Washington coast to fish with your father for ten years now, and I know very little about you. I've virtually watched you grow up, yet you're so quiet, so self-contained, that you're still a mystery to me.'

'Look,' she said, suddenly wearying of the cat-and-mouse game he was playing with her. 'I don't know what you want from me. I'm only here listening to you at all because of the mess my father's got himself into. Just tell me what it is you want, and let's get this farce over with.'

'But I have already told you what I wanted,' he said smoothly. There was only one lamp burning in the room, on her side of the sofa, and his face was in the shadows so that she couldn't make out his expression. 'What I want,' he continued, 'is for you to tell me about yourself. It's a simple enough request.'

'I don't understand you,' she said. 'There's nothing to tell. There's nothing about me a man like you would find the least interesting—or entertaining.'

'You let me worry about your—ah—entertainment value.' He settled back on the cushions and crossed one ankle over his knee. 'Have you always lived in Southport?'

'Yes.'

'How old are you?'

'Twenty-four.'

'You keep house, cook for your father and brothers? Handle the books?

She nodded. Good Lord, she thought, he sounded like an employer interviewing her. Was he going to offer her a job? 'And take care of my mother,' she added softly.

'Yes, of course. She's quite ill, your father tells me. Cancer. She must suffer a lot.'

Dumbly, miserably, Cara nodded. It was one subject she had no intention of discussing with this man. She was in his power, at his mercy, but she would not allow him to see into her heart or gauge the depth of her feelings.

He kept on questioning her for another half hour. She answered him briefly and succinctly, but volunteered nothing. Had she ever been married? No. Engaged? No. She was obviously intelligent and articulate. Where had she gone to school? The Sacred Heart, a convent school. What did she do in her spare time? She replied shortly that she had no spare time now that her mother was bedridden, but she used to read a lot and enjoyed music, walking on the beach. When the question and answer session was over, he was silent for a long time.

Then, softly, he said, 'Your father tells me that at one time you wanted very much to be a nun.'

Cara's mind closed shut. 'I don't discuss that with anyone,' she snapped. 'Especially you.'

'But it's over?' he persisted gently.

'It's over,' she said curtly.

There was another long silence. He seemed to be deep in thought, his face expressionless. Cara watched him warily. He was gazing into space, his face turned to her in profile. She had never really looked at him before, she thought, never really noticed him. In the past he had been only one of her father's passengers, arriving each year, fishing for a week, and then leaving again until the next year. Now, in just a few short days, he had become her enemy, with enormous power over her and her family.

But what kind of man was he? She supposed he would be called handsome. His features were regular, with a straight, rather long nose, a firm chin, the hollows of his cheeks somewhat gaunt. His dark hair was well-cut and neatly combed. A reserved, secretive man, she thought, with an air of lean asceticism about him. She might almost take him for a monk if she didn't know his real character and background.

He turned to her abruptly, and she quickly looked away. Remember, she warned herself, he is not a monk. He is the enemy.

'So,' he said at last, 'what do you want from life, Cara? You're an enigma to me. I've never met anyone quite like you. A well-educated girl who went to a country school run by nuns. A poised, composed, cool lady who spends her days waiting on four clods and tending a dying mother. A beautiful, desirable woman who's never even been in love.' He leaned forward and narrowed his eyes. 'Tell me, Cara,' he demanded in a low, tense tone. 'What is it you want?'

She returned his gaze fully. 'Nothing at all that you could offer me,' she replied in a cool, clear voice. 'Now, are you through with me? May I please go?'

She started to rise up, but a hand shot out and clamped her hard around the forearm. 'I'm not through,' he ground out.

'Take your hand off me,' she said in a tight voice. Anger rose up within her, simmering just below the surface. The touch of his hand on her arm made her flesh crawl. 'You've had your fun, now let me go.'

'No,' he barked. 'I'm not through with you.'

She stared at him. The hooded eyes were menacing and the hungry look on his face frightened her. 'What is it you want from me?' she whispered.

He was on his feet now, his hand still on her arm, pulling her up, the strong fingers biting into her soft flesh. With his free hand, he grasped her throat and forced her head back so that she had to look up into those glittering eyes. His touch was quite firm, but oddly gentle.

'I'll tell you what I want, Cara,' he murmured. 'I want you.'

She exhaled slowly, and it seemed as though all the breath had gone out of her body. There it was, then, she thought stoically, exactly what she had feared earlier and dismissed as irrational. Her mind raced beneath her calm exterior. She clenched her fists at her sides, her fingernails digging into the palms of her hands, her arms rigid, trying to still her pounding heart and clear her head so that she could think. Not by a flicker of an eyelash did she want to betray the turmoil raging within her to this unspeakable man.

She gazed unflinchingly into the steely eyes above her, and when she saw the naked desire flashing now in the silver depths, a sudden icy calm filled her at the realisation that for some inexplicable reason, she had a strange, unbidden power over him. When she spoke, her voice was steady, without a tremor.

'If you'll quit choking me, why don't we sit down and talk about it,' she said calmly.

The grey eyes widened momentarily in surprise, then a slow smile spread across his face, and the hand at her throat relaxed its hold. For a moment it hesitated, lingering there, then abruptly he removed it.

'You're the most amazing woman I've ever met, Cara O'Neal,' he murmured. 'And I've known quite a few.' He shook his head slowly from side to side. 'I've never known one like you, however.'

He drew her down beside him then, and took his hand off her arm. They sat there quietly for a moment, close but not touching, while Cara framed her next question in her mind. She knew instinctively that in order to deal with this man she must not show a flicker of fear.

'Just exactly what is it you want?' she asked slowly.

'I told you,' he responded immediately. 'I want you.'

She frowned. 'I heard that part,' she said drily. 'Now I'd like to know why and on what terms.' Her mouth crooked into a rueful parody of a smile. 'You'll have to forgive me for my incredulity, but I'm well aware of the fact that I'm not your average everyday *femme fatale*. I'm more than a little surprised that you consider my—whatever it is you want—worth bargaining over.'

She glanced down at her shabby grey woollen skirt, the worn loafers on her feet, the simple white shirt and loose dark green cardigan.

'I know you don't understand,' he said, 'and your lack of awareness of your—ah—charms and attributes is a good deal of your appeal.' He narrowed his eyes at her. 'Let's just say that you happen to be what I'm looking for in a woman. If you really need a reason, I can only tell you that I've watched you for years, seen you grow from a coltish young girl into a poised, beautiful woman. With all your efforts to hide it under those hideous clothes, you have a body that set me on fire the moment I laid eyes on you.' He reached out then and traced a finger along the line of her collarbone under her cotton shirt. 'I love the way you move,'

he went on in a low, murmuring voice. 'So stiff
and proud, but with a fluid grace a queen would
envy.' With his finger he moved her chin so that
she was looking straight at him. 'I want to get lost
in those emerald eyes of yours, take down that
thick mane of black hair and let it run through my
fingers . . .'

'That's enough!' Cara cried in a low voice,
drawing away from him. It sickened her to hear
such words coming from him. No one had ever
spoken to her like that before. 'I don't believe a
word of it, but whatever your reasons are, you do
hold all the cards. I'll do just about anything to get
my father out of this mess he's got us into, and
you know that quite well. So just tell me what
your terms are, and I'll see if I can tolerate what
you ask.'

He leaned back against the arm of the sofa and
folded his arms across his chest. 'All right, Cara,'
he said quietly. 'I'll tell you what my terms are. I'll
tear up the notes your father gave me for the two
boats. I'll also arrange for the best housekeeping
and nursing care for your mother—or for
hospitalisation in Reno, if you'd prefer.'

'In Reno?' What was he talking about? 'Why
Reno?'

'Because that's where the closest hospital to
Lake Tahoe is located.'

'And what's at Lake Tahoe?' she asked,
dreading what was coming.

'My home,' was the prompt reply. He fixed his
glittering eyes on her, bending closer.

She had already anticipated the worst, and his
calm pronouncement came as no real surprise to
her. Now she had to decide if she could go

through with it. She lifted her chin and gazed at him.

'And for how long is this—this arrangement of yours to last?'

He chuckled. 'For life, Cara. I want you to marry me.'

CHAPTER TWO

'YOU'VE got to be joking!' she breathed. At his totally unexpected words she had shrunk back from him. 'You're insane.'

He shook his head. 'Oh, no, Cara. Not insane. I know exactly what I'm doing.' His mouth twisted sardonically. 'Don't look so shocked. You were prepared to sleep with me. I'm offering you a respectable alternative.'

She could only stare at him in stunned disbelief. She didn't want to marry anyone, had never intended, never visualised such a prospect in her future. Once she had given up all hope of the one thing she really wanted, that future had simply ceased to exist for her. She had made up her mind then, six years ago, that she would live one day at a time, do what had to be done, and perhaps one day the sisters might take her after all.

For as long as she could remember, Cara had wanted to join the Sacred Heart sisters in their convent overlooking the sea, those calm, serene nuns who had instilled in her such a love of learning, of the beauties of art and nature, and a simple self-respect. As the youngest child in a family of men, she had been looked upon as nothing more than a servant by her father and brothers, and the nuns had taught her that human dignity was possible no matter what one's circumstances.

When she had first requested admission as a

novice, she had been barely eighteen. She would never forget her disappointment when the kindly prioress had turned her down, telling her she was too young and inexperienced to make such a critical decision, advising her to try to get more education, to leave the village, to learn more about life before she committed herself so irrevocably.

Then, a year later, her mother had been sticken with the cancer that was slowly killing her and there was no question of her leaving home. She had stayed on. She had no choice.

She turned again to the strange, dark man beside her. It was like a dream. 'Why?' she whispered.

'I explained all that,' he said with a shrug of his broad shoulders. 'You strike me as a woman without an ounce of vanity, but if you like I'll go back and enumerate my reasons for you again.'

'No,' she said wryly, recovering herself. 'I understand that part. I know you want me, and I think I know why.' She gave him a cool look. 'I'm a novelty to you. You said it yourself. The village virgin. But why marriage? It seems a little drastic.'

'Would you have come to me as my mistress?' he asked softly.

She thought it over. 'I'm not sure,' she said at last. 'I hadn't decided.'

'I didn't think so. So, aside from the fact that I'm thirty-six years old and have been thinking for some time of marrying, settling down, having a family, there is also the fact that I want you any way I can get you. You're what I want.'

'And you always get what you want.'

He nodded briefly. 'Just about.'

It was almost funny, Cara thought. She had just

about convinced herself to sleep with him, be his mistress for—what? A week or two? A month? Until he tired of her, at any rate. But marriage! To a man like Nicholas Curzon? She knew hardly anything about him, and what she did know appalled her. First, he was ready to ruin her father over a card game, and now he was proposing to purchase her as he would a horse or a head of cattle.

'Well?' he said at last. 'What's your answer?'

She turned her cool green gaze on him. 'Not in a million years, Mr Curzon,' she said calmly. She stood up, pleased to see the dull red flush that covered his arrogant, self-assured face. 'Now, will you please leave this house?'

With catlike grace, he sprang to his feet and stood looking down at her. A pulse was beating wildly along his jawline just under his ear, and she enjoyed her moment of triumph over him.

'Yes,' he ground out. 'I'll go. But you'll change your mind. And when you do, you'll have to come to me. I'm leaving tomorrow at noon, either with you or with the bill of sale on your father's boats. It's up to you.' And with his cold voice still ringing in her ears, she watched him stride away from her.

It wasn't until he was gone, the front door closed firmly behind him, and she heard the sound of his departing footsteps on the porch, that Cara let go. She closed her eyes and reached out to clutch the back of a chair, trembling and shivering. She felt faint and dizzy. Her mind was simply unable to grasp the enormity of what had occurred.

She stood there for what seemed like hours. As her head cleared gradually and the quaking tremors passed, she began to realise that even though she had been unequivocally firm in her refusal of Nicholas Curzon's fantastic proposal, it was by no means the end of the affair. She knew very little about the man, but her instinct told her that the one thing he would never do was back down from an ultimatum.

He was a gambler, wasn't he? She had seen it in the cold grey eyes. He meant what he said. If she didn't marry him, he would take the boats, she knew it, and do so without a pang of remorse or guilt.

Her thoughts were broken by the sound of footsteps coming down the stairs. She turned to see her father shuffling into the room, an expectant, hopeful light in his eyes.

'Well?' he said coming towards her.

She watched him carefully as he approached and was startled to see a shamefaced look flicker over the weatherbeaten face. She knew then what all the shouting had been about before dinner that evening.

'You knew,' she said flatly. He lowered his eyes. 'Oh, Dad, how could you?'

'What did you tell him?' he asked in a low, choked voice.

'I refused him, of course.'

His expression hardened. 'Now look here, Cara,' he said fiercely. 'No one's going to force you into anything. But just stop and think a minute. Forget the boats. Forget the business. Think of yourself. It's the opportunity of a lifetime for you.' His voice softened, wheedling. 'He's a rich man, Cara. He can give you anything you want.'

She stared at him. 'No. You're wrong. He can't.
I don't believe you, Dad. Are you seriously
suggesting that I sell myself to this man—for life?'
She shook her head. 'No, Dad. I won't do it. We'll
find a way to keep the boats, at least one of them.
We'll get by. You'll see.'

A look of utter defeat passed over his face. He
ran a hand over his untidy grey hair and sighed. 'I
can see there's no arguing with you when your
mind's made up,' he said at last. Then, to her
astonishment, he smiled crookedly. 'You always
were a stubborn girl. Can't imagine where you got
it.'

'Oh, Dad,' she said, near to tears at the
unaccustomed gentleness, and took a step towards
him.

He patted her awkwardly on the shoulder. 'Go
on, now,' he said gruffly. 'Your mother wants
you.'

'Have you told her?' He nodded. 'Everything?'
He nodded again.

She went up to her mother's room, then, and
stood in the doorway. A dim light was burning
beside the bed. Her mother was propped up on a
pillow with her eyes closed.

'Mother?' Cara said softly, walking towards her.

The eyes fluttered open, and she smiled weakly.
'Sit down, Cara. I want to talk to you.'

'Dad said he told you—everything,' Cara said as
she sat down carefully on the edge of the bed. 'I
wish he hadn't.'

'I don't see why not,' the sick woman said with
spirit. 'I'm not feeble-minded, you know.'

Cara smiled and took her mother's hand. 'I
know. Far from it.'

After a short silence, her mother said, 'Mr Curzon wants you to marry him.' It was a flat statement.

'Yes.'

'Are you going to?'

'No.'

'Why not?'

Cara's eyes widened. 'Why not? How can you ask? I loathe the man. He's a monster.'

'But you don't even know him.'

'I know enough to convince me he's the last man on earth I'd marry.'

The frail hand tightened on Cara's and, gazing at her intently, the sick woman said, 'Don't worry about the business, Cara. We'll manage. We've never taken charity in our lives, but it's there if we need it. It's you I'm thinking of.' She was silent for a moment, then went on. 'I want you to get out of here, Cara. Out of this house, out of Southport. You're wasted here.'

'Oh, Mother,' Cara objected, but the sick woman raised a hand.

'You care about me, don't you, Cara?'

'Of course. How can you ask?'

'Then do this thing for me. At least think about it. Don't reject it without giving it serious consideration. And don't blame Mr Curzon. I know how foolish your father can be. He told me himself that it was his own fault he lost the boats.'

'But I don't want to marry at all,' Cara protested.

Her mother nodded. 'I know that. I know you, too. What would you have agreed to do to help your father?' She fixed her daughter with a penetrating gaze.

Cara's eyes fell under that knowing look. 'I'm not sure,' she mumbled.

'Well, I am. I think you would have agreed to almost anything.'

Cara could only stare at her. 'All right. Yes. You're right. I would have agreed to be his mistress for a time. But marriage! What kind of man . . .'

'An honourable man!' her mother snapped. 'Have you considered that possibility? Perhaps this offer of marriage means that he wants to save you the pain of prostituting yourself.'

Cara winced at the harsh word. She hadn't considered that interpretation of his motives, and didn't really give it much credence now. Still, she owed it to her mother to think it over carefully. She stood up now and straightened the covers around the thin form.

'I'll think about it, Mother,' she said. 'I promise I'll think it over.'

'That's all I ask, Cara.' She closed her eyes, then, and the tense features relaxed.

Cara switched off the lamp and tiptoed quietly out of the room. The odd conversation with her mother had confused her, shaken her firm conviction that never, under any circumstances, could she marry Nicholas Curzon.

She slept very little that night as she pondered the matter over and over again in her mind. Perhaps her mother was right. Not for a minute did she believe the man's intentions had anything to do with her welfare, however. For reasons of his own he wanted a wife, wanted her, and when the opportunity to get what he wanted presented itself, he simply reached out and took it.

Cara knew, however, that much as she despised him and everything he stood for, her wishes, her welfare, weren't the only things that mattered. Other people were involved here, her mother, most of all, and she had been firm in urging her to marry the man. There were also her brothers to consider, Patrick especially. Could she ever forgive herself if, being the sole means of her whole family's salvation, she refused to do the one thing that would ensure it?

Besides that, her mother was right. There was no future for her here in Southport, nothing at all she really wanted. She might just as well throw herself away on Nicholas Curzon, and help her family in the process, as rot here in certain poverty.

She finally fell into a troubled sleep, and when she awoke the next morning, her mind was made up. She knew what she had to do.

'Mr Nicholas Curzon's room, please,' she said into the telephone.

While she waited for him to answer, she went over her speech again, the speech she had been practising ever since breakfast. Once she had accepted the fact that she was really going to do it, a strange calm had settled on her. It was now eleven-thirty. She had waited until the last minute to call him. Let him wonder, she had decided coldly.

'Nicholas Curzon,' came the deep voice.

'This is Cara O'Neal, Mr Curzon,' she said quietly. 'I've changed my mind. If you still want to marry me, I'll agree.'

In the sudden silence she thought she heard him

pull in his breath sharply, but when he spoke his voice was cool and controlled, with no trace of emotion.

'I see,' he said at last. 'What changed your mind?'

'I don't care to go into my reasons,' she replied curtly. 'Is the offer still open or not?'

'Well, since you put it so charmingly, how can I resist? Yes, the offer is still open. I'll be right over.'

Before she could protest, he had hung up the 'phone. She hadn't expected that. She sighed deeply and replaced the receiver in its cradle. She knew she'd have to face him sooner or later. She had hoped to have more time.

But what difference did it make, she thought as she went into the kitchen to start her mother's lunch. It was probably best to get it over with right away. Leave it to him, she thought, to pounce the moment he saw an advantage.

The motel where he was staying was only three blocks away, and in just a few minutes she heard his step on the wooden porch. The doorbell rang. She turned the burner down under the soup she was heating and went to answer it, steeling herself for their meeting.

When she opened the door, it was as though she was confronted with a stranger. He was dressed in a conservative dark blue suit, a white shirt and a muted silk paisley tie. The clothes were obviously expensive, even to her inexperienced eye, and gave him an air of assurance and authority that was powerful in its impact. He was quite tall, over six feet, she guessed, looking up at him, and his height gave him an added advantage.

'May I come in?' he asked politely.

She moved back a step and opened the door wider to let him pass. He stepped inside, and as she closed the door behind him, her heart began to pound in nervous anticipation. She was determined, however, not to let him see how agitated she was.

He turned around and smiled at her. 'Well, Cara—I assume now that we're officially engaged you have no objection to the name,' he remarked drily. 'I'd like to leave as soon as possible.'

Cara's hopes soared. Any delay meant that much more time to look for an alternative. 'You still plan to leave today at noon?' she asked. It was almost that time now.

He shook his head. 'No. We'll drive up to Gray's Harbor today, apply for a licence and be married the statutory three days later. A few more days won't make that much difference, but the sooner I get back to Reno the better. You'll fly back with me.'

Cara's heart sank. 'That's not possible.'

'Why not?' he shot back. 'That's time enough to organise things, isn't it?'

Cara put a hand to her throat. 'No ... no ... it's ... I can't be ready to leave so soon.'

His glance flicked over her. She had deliberately dressed in her shabbiest blue jeans, tennis shoes and a shapeless grey pullover of Patrick's. She wore no make-up and had pulled her hair back in its usual careless knot.

'If you mean clothes,' he drawled, 'as women so often do, we can pick up a few things in Gray's Harbor and fill in the rest when we get to Reno.'

'That isn't what I meant, and I think you'll find that I'm not at all like the women you know. Not about clothes. Not about anything else.'

The grey eyes gleamed and he took a step towards her. 'Oh, I'm well aware of that, Cara. Why else do you think I want you?'

She refused to back away from him. 'There's one thing I'd like to make quite clear, Mr Curzon.'

'Nicholas,' he murmured.

'Very well. Nicholas, then.' He was so close to her now that she could see the fine weave of the soft woollen jacket he wore, smell the fresh cool masculine scent of him, a hint of tobacco and soap, and it was all she could do not to step back. 'As far as I'm concerned, your offer of marriage in exchange for the boats is a business proposition I couldn't in conscience turn down. Those were your terms, but I have a few of my own.'

His face hardened. 'Understand one thing, Cara. This is going to be a marriage in every sense of the word.'

'I didn't for one minute think otherwise,' she returned coldly. 'My opinion of you is too low to imagine that you would deny yourself any of the rights you had paid for out of consideration for me.'

He didn't even flinch. 'It's not your opinions I'm interested in, believe me.'

'No. Of course not. But I do have some rights, and before we go through with this farce, I want you to understand my terms clearly.'

'And what are they?'

'First of all, I'm to choose my own clothes. I won't have you dressing me up like a tart and parading me in front of your fellow . . . thugs.'

He winced slightly. 'Is that how you think of me? As a thug?'

She shrugged. 'How I really think of you wouldn't bear repeating. Do you agree or not?'

'About the clothes? Of course. I don't care what you wear. I doubt, however, that you'll feel comfortable among my friends in an outfit like the one you have on.'

'Perhaps not, but it's to be my choice.' He nodded his agreement. 'Second,' she went on, 'I'm to be allowed to come home to visit my family whenever I want.'

'Within reason, of course,' he replied. 'It's not my intention to keep you prisoner, Cara. I want a wife not a slave.'

'In my mind there's not a particle of difference.' She expected an angry retort to that, but he only set his jaw more firmly and continued to gaze down at her. She was impressed in spite of herself with his patience. Any other man would have walked out the door or been shouting at her long ago.

'Is that all?' he asked.

'No. There's one more thing.' She lifted her chin. We'll see now just how far his patience goes. 'I'm to have my own bedroom.'

His face darkened at that, and the pulse in his jaw began to pound again. He narrowed his eyes at her. 'I told you this was going to be a marriage in every sense of the word, and I meant it. Make no mistake about that. You are going to be my wife, in my house, at my table, and in my bed.'

'I understand that,' she said, 'all too well. I have no intention of refusing you any of your marital rights. That doesn't mean I have to enjoy it, however. I'll need a place that is my own, inviolable. If I can't have that place, the agreement is off.'

They stood there with their eyes locked together for several moments, neither giving an inch. Cara's mind was made up quite firmly on this. She could endure living with him, even sharing his bed, but she had to have a private retreat that belonged to her alone.

Finally, he nodded. 'All right. I'll agree to that—temporarily, anyway—on the condition that you make yourself available to me whenever I want you.'

'I've already told you I would.'

He folded his arms across his chest then, and slowly shook his head from side to side. 'I was right about you,' he said. 'You're more than a match for any man. It will give me more pleasure than you can ever know to tame you, Cara O'Neal.'

She laughed shortly. 'It will never happen.'

He smiled. 'We'll see,' he murmured, and before she realised what he was doing, he had reached out and put his arms around her, pulling her closely up against him.

When she felt the strength of his firm embrace, she knew there was no hope of fighting him, and she held herself rigidly in his arms. When she felt his grip relax and his hands move up over her arms, her shoulders, she shuddered involuntarily at his touch on her body.

He placed the palms of his hands on either side of her face then, and tilted her head back so that she was forced to look up at him. The grey eyes were surprisingly gentle, and his thumbs began to move slowly over her mouth.

'Don't fight me, Cara,' he murmured. 'I don't want to harm you in any way.'

Then, as she stared, his head came down and she felt his cool lips pressing on hers, lightly at first, then more firmly as his arms came around her again and held her closely against his lean, hard frame. As the kiss deepened and became more demanding, she felt the tip of his tongue against her lips seeking entrance.

Startled, she clamped her mouth firmly shut and tried to pull away from him, but he held her tight.

'Open your mouth to me, Cara,' he muttered against her lips.

She jerked her head back. 'No,' she cried, and looked up at him with hatred flashing in her green eyes. She placed her hands on his chest and levered herself some space away from him. 'When we're married,' she said evenly, 'I'll be your property and you can do what you like with me. Until then, I'm my own person, and I have the right to make that decision.'

A shutter came down over the grey eyes, and he dropped his arms to his sides. 'Then the sooner we get it done the better,' he ground out. 'I'm a patient man, Cara, but not beyond a certain point. It will give me great pleasure to penetrate that icy reserve of yours. Now, go change your clothes. We're going to Gray's Harbor to apply for that licence, and we'll get married as soon as we can be.

Four days later Cara sat on a plane next to her new husband on her way to Nevada. She stared out the window, hardly able to take it all in, everything had happened so fast.

They had been married in the living room of the cottage so that her mother could attend. Through the intervention of the nuns, who, amazingly, approved of the odd situation, the parish priest had been persuaded to perform the simple ceremony on such short notice. That afternoon they had driven to Seattle in Nicholas's rental car to catch their plane to Reno.

It was Cara's first airplane trip, and in spite of her inner turmoil and dread anticipation of what lay ahead for her as the wife of Nicholas Curzon, she was almost childishly excited at the novelty of flying several thousand feet above the ground. She could even forget for a few precious moments the fact that she was now bound legally to a virtual stranger.

It was a beautiful, clear day, crisp with the promise of fall. Down below, Mount Rainier rose up in majestic isolation, sparkling white in the sunlight, its snow-covered peak towering above the surrounding mountains of the Cascade Range. Just ahead lay Mount St Helen's, its still-steaming volcanic crater a black gash in the centre from its recent eruptions.

Then, suddenly, they were flying through a white mist. The plane nosed upward, and the terrain of the ground below vanished, to be replaced by a soft, fluffy layer of clouds, gleaming blindingly in the bright sunshine still overhead.

Cara blinked. It was like a fairyland. She'd never seen anything like it. It was as though the earth had vanished and they were floating in a different universe where all familiar points of reference were gone and everything was clean and new.

She felt a touch on her arm. Without thinking, she turned to the man beside her, her eyes wide, a

smile on her face. The hand on her arm tightened,
and he leaned across her to look out the window
so that his face was only inches away from hers.

'Are you frightened?' he asked in a low tone.

At the sound of his voice, she was suddenly
jolted back into reality and instinctively shrank
back in her seat away from him. The magic of the
scene outside was gone, and the dull ache in her
heart returned.

'Of course not,' she snapped. 'Should I be?'

Slowly he eased away from her and withdrew
the hand on her arm. 'It's your first plane trip,' he
said distantly. 'I thought you might need some
reassurance that the earth hadn't vanished. These
cloud banks can be rather unsettling if you've
never flown over them before.'

'I see,' she said evenly. 'Thank you for your
concern. It never occurred to me that my feelings
were even remotely interesting to you.'

To her surprise, he only smiled at the sharp
comment. 'You know, Cara,' he said in a lazy
conversational tone, 'you're only hurting yourself
with that attitude. How long are you going to keep
it up?'

She gazed directly at him. 'Probably for as long
as this—marriage—lasts. If you can call it that.'

He merely shrugged and turned away from her,
leaning his head back and closing his eyes. His
refusal to react to her baiting annoyed her. She
wanted to wound him, make him angry, even
incite him to violence. Anything to wipe that smug
self-satisfied smirk off his face.

'Tell me something,' she said. He opened his
eyes halfway and glanced over at her. 'I'm a little
concerned about my duties as the consort of a

gambling impresario. Will I have to entertain a lot
of gangsters? The Mafia, perhaps?'

The grey eyes flew open, and he sat up straight
in his seat. 'Of course not,' was the sharp reply.
'Just what do you think I am?'

'I have no idea. I know nothing about you.'

'What do you want to know?'

'Nothing,' she replied tightly. 'I just want my
duties spelled out a little more clearly so I'll know
what to expect.'

The lids came down again. 'You're an intelligent
woman. You'll learn fast.' Again a lazy smile
appeared on his face. 'Tonight I'll teach you the
most important of your duties. Fighting me will
only make it harder for you.'

Before she could reply, he had settled back in
his seat and closed his eyes again. He seemed to
fall instantly asleep, and as she watched him, the
steady rise and fall of his chest under the dark blue
suit, his even breathing, her anger began to drain
slowly away.

He was right, she thought sadly. The harder she
fought, the worse she would make the situation for
herself. What was the point? She had committed
herself. He was a hard man, even a ruthless one,
but from the little she had seen of him, he didn't
seem cruel.

She thought about the clothes shopping he had
insisted she do in Gray's Harbor when they'd gone
to apply for the marriage licence at the County
Courthouse. He had tried to give her money, but
when she had firmly refused, determined to use her
own meagre savings to buy the inexpensive
wedding dress and travelling suit, he hadn't
pushed her.

She had deliberately chosen a starkly simple black dress to be married in, but when she appeared at his side this morning at the wedding, he had barely raised an eyebrow at her funereal attire.

She dreaded her wedding night above all else. She was confident she could handle the rest of her duties competently in time, but the thought of lying in this man's bed with his hands on her, possessing her, simply didn't bear thinking about. Her experience with men, outside her father and brothers, was virtually zero. Her intention had been to keep it that way. The men in the village, mostly rough fishermen, didn't remotely interest her, even though several had tried to push past her icy reserve. Now her first intimate experience with a man would be with her worst enemy.

CHAPTER THREE

IT was early evening when the plane touched down in Reno, and even though the small city was pretty much as she had expected, she still wasn't prepared to come upon the sudden blaze of lights glaring in the darkening sky after seeing nothing but miles of black wilderness down below for so long.

Nestled in the foothills of the rugged Sierra Nevada mountains that made a natural boundary between the states of California and Nevada, the town was surrounded by forest. It was with a feeling of unreality that Cara got off the plane and walked beside Nicholas into the small terminal to collect their baggage and then out to the car, a sleek silver Mercedes that he had left in the parking lot while he was in Southport.

As they drove through the town, she stared in amazement at the brightly lit casinos and hotels that sprang up on every side, neon lights blinking, crowds of people milling about the narrow streets. There was a decided holiday atmosphere—'The Biggest Little City in the World' proclaimed a sign stretched high across the main street—and Cara wondered if people actually lived there. Somehow it seemed to her that the population must be made up entirely of tourists who came and went interchangeably.

Yet, Nicholas lived there, she thought as they drove slowly through the crowded centre of town, and so must all the others who served the holiday gamblers. And now, it suddenly struck her with a little inward shiver of apprehension, so would she.

Without turning her head, she glanced sideways at the man seated next to her, wondering for the first time what kind of man he was beneath that smooth, controlled, confident exterior. Everything had happened so fast that she hadn't had a moment to really consider what her life would be like as the wife of Nicholas Curzon. Ever since she had first found out about her father losing the boats to him, a sense of unreality had possessed her. She had made her decision to marry him, bought the new clothes, applied for the marriage licence, gone through a wedding ceremony and bid her family goodbye as though she were playing a part in a drama or walking through a dream.

Now, the reality of her situation began to encroach inexorably on her consciousness, and with it came some very real qualms about what she had done. At the time, it had seemed the only logical thing to do, especially when her mother had urged her so strongly. Now she wasn't so sure. Glancing surreptitiously at him again, she thought, he could be a wife-beater, a pervert, even a criminal. He seemed not to notice her scrutiny, and his eyes were fixed firmly on the road ahead as he drove.

He didn't *look* like a criminal, she thought, but then, how would she know what a criminal looked like? His dark good looks were impressive, and she guessed that most women would find him very attractive. But then why did he find it necessary to *buy* a wife? Cara had never gone an inch out of her way to attract him or any other man, and she had no illusions about her seductive power. Why, then, did this man want her badly enough to exchange the two boats he had won from her father for her promise of marriage? There had to be a reason, and she was almost afraid to find out what it was.

They were outside the city, now, on a wide smooth highway, following the high ridge of the mountain range to their right and leaving the bright lights behind them. Where were they? Where were they going? She turned to him.

'I thought you lived in Reno,' she said in a tight voice.

'He gave her a brief, amused glance. 'No. My business is in Reno. I live at Lake Tahoe.'

They had barely spoken since the plane landed, and they continued on in silence now. Soon they started up a curved road that seemed to lead directly into the heart of the tall mountains looming black against the night sky. Finally, in the distance, more lights appeared, the road straightened out, and they were driving along another brilliantly lit street lined with hotels and casinos.

'Are you cold?' Nicholas asked.

'A little.'

'It's the elevation. We get quite a bit of snow here later on.' He reached out to the dashboard, turned a switch and soon warm air filled the interior of the car.

Now they seemed to be in a quiet residential area. He stopped the car at an iron gate set in a solid brick wall and reached across her into the glove compartment. She heard a slight humming sound as the gate opened, and they drove through on to a narrower paved road that curved around to the front of a house, which, even in the darkness, looked large and imposing. He pulled up in front of it and shut off the engine. For a moment, there was absolute silence. Then he turned to her.

'Well, we're home.'

Before she could reply, he had got out of the car, crossed around in front and opened her door. Slowly, she stepped out and stood shivering in the darkness, which was broken only by a few lights coming from the house.

Nicholas went to the boot of the car to get their baggage, and while she waited for him Cara stared at her new home. It was a low, rambling structure and seemed to spread out endlessly. He's a rich man, her father had said. Now she believed him. The luxurious car, the expensive clothes he wore, this sprawling house, all bespoke money.

'Let's go in,' he said at her side. 'It's cold out here.'

She followed him down a wide path surrounded by lawns and dark shrubbery to a low, covered portico. There were gleaming double doors flanked by yellowish lights, a brass knocker. Nicholas set the bags down and reached in his pocket for his keys, but just then the door opened and a tall, grey-haired woman dressed in black stood before them.

When she saw Nicholas, her eyes lit up. 'Welcome home, Mr Curzon.'

'Thank you, Mrs Varga,' he said, and they stepped inside a wide entrance hall paved with red quarry tiles. He set the bags down. 'This is my wife, Mrs Varga.' He turned to Cara. 'My housekeeper, Mrs Varga.'

The two women nodded at each other.

'Welcome, Mrs Curzon,' the tall woman said. If she was surprised at the news that her employer had returned home with a wife in tow, she didn't reveal it by so much as a flicker of an eyelash. 'I hope you had a pleasant trip.'

'Thank you,' Cara murmured. A housekeeper! What in the world was she supposed to do with a housekeeper? They at least should have a lot in common, she thought wryly, since that's what she had been herself for so many years.

Wordlessly, she followed Nicholas and Mrs Varga down the long hall, past an enormous living room where a fire was burning in a massive stone fireplace, then past several other doors and down another narrower hallway to the back of the house.

Nicholas stopped at a closed door and turned to the housekeeper. 'We'll clean up now, Mrs Varga, and get unpacked. Could you have a little supper ready for us, say, in an hour?'

He glanced enquiringly at Cara. Food, she thought, appalled, and her stomach turned over. 'I'm not very hungry,' she murmured.

Mrs Varga nodded and walked back down the hall. Nicholas opened the door and switched on the light, then stood back to let Cara precede him into the room.

'This will be your room,' he said, setting her bags down on the bed. 'For now. It's really a guest room and has its own bathroom.' He set a large parcel he had been carrying down on the bed beside her suitcases. 'I bought that for you while we were in Gray's Harbor the other day,' he said, his voice casual. 'I'd like to have you wear it tonight.' He was staring at her, but she barely heard him, and when she made no reply, he went back to the door. 'I'm just across the hall if you need me. Otherwise, I'll stop by for you in an hour.'

When he was gone, Cara stood in the middle of the room and gazed around her. It was larger than all the bedrooms in her parents' house put together, softly carpeted in a light greyish-green colour, the walls covered with a rough natural linen fabric. On the large double bed was a quilted spread in the same colour a few shades darker, as were the draperies at the windows. It was rich, elegant and subdued, like a photograph in a glossy magazine.

If Cara had felt disorientated before, she was simply stunned now. She'd had no idea Nicholas Curzon lived in such a home. Somehow she had pictured him in a more ornate setting, with scarlet wallpaper, a lot of cheap gilt, mirrors everywhere, certainly a more glamorous, flamboyant decor than the understated richness of what she had seen so far.

She wanted very much to be alone, but she knew he had no intention of letting her spend their wedding night by herself. And nothing on earth would induce her to beg. She'd made her bed, literally, and now she'd have to lie in it.

The bathroom was tiled in the same grey-green, the fixtures a creamy muted yellow. Thick towels hung neatly on the racks, and there was an assortment of bath oils, powders and soap on the marble counter over the washbasin. She looked longingly at the sparkling bath. A bath is what I need, she thought, a long hot soak.

While the water ran in the bath, she hurriedly

unpacked her overnight case, where she had
placed everything she would need tonight. She
would get at the large suitcase, which contained
the rest of her meagre wardrobe, tomorrow. As
she took her things out of the case, her eye fell
on the package Nicholas had left on the bed.
She had a good idea what was in it, and could
just imagine what *he* would choose for her to
wear tonight.

Of course, she thought bitterly. He would want
to humiliate her as much as possible this first
night, set the tone for the future, show her who
was master right from the start. Well, he had
already agreed that she had the right to choose her
own clothes, and she had certain boundaries of her
own she intended to set tonight, too.

She took out one of her own worn cotton
nightgowns from her case and the dark blue
woollen robe Patrick had given her for Christmas
three years ago, the same one she had worn ever
since. Nicholas Curzon could keep whatever
revealing négligé he had taken it upon himself to
buy for her. She wasn't going to put on a floor
show for him.

After soaking in the steaming bath for almost
half an hour, and dressed now in her own gown,
her own robe, Cara felt her spirits revive. She was
still somewhat apprehensive about her future,
especially this first night, but as she brushed her
long thick hair in front of the dressing-table
mirror, her courage gradually began to return. All
she had to do was to obey Nicholas Curzon in the
areas where he had already staked his claim, but
for the rest she was determined to do as she
pleased, to fight him every inch of the way and to

resist every incursion into her privacy except what he had already paid for.

While she pinned her hair back up, her glance fell again and again on the parcel still lying on the bed unopened. Finally, her curiosity won out, and she walked over to it. Quickly, she untied the string and opened the box, pushing aside the layers of tissue paper until she saw what was inside.

She couldn't believe her eyes. Slowly, she took out the white gown and held it up. It was made of the finest, softest handkerchief linen, very simple, very plain, except for a wide square-necked yoke of obviously handmade lace. It was simply exquisite, and not in the least what she had expected. As she ran her hands over the silky material, tears came to her eyes. If this had been a real marriage, she thought sadly, if she were waiting here now for a man she loved, a man who loved and respected her, this was exactly the gown she would have chosen to wear.

Instead she was waiting for a man she detested, a man who had literally purchased her, on a whim, as he would a pet dog. Angrily, she let the gown drop back into its box, hating the sight of it now. She carried it to the wardrobe and pushed it far back on the shelf.

There was a light knock on the door, and her heart sank. She turned around and pulled the belt of her robe more tightly around her, staring at the door. She couldn't move, couldn't make her feet walk those few steps to open it or force any sound from her dry throat.

I should have put on a dress, she thought. Was it too late? What am I doing standing here in my nightgown and robe with that *stranger* waiting for me on the other side? The knock came again, louder this time. She continued to stand there, frozen, her heart pounding deafeningly in her ears.

'Cara,' came his voice at last. 'Are you all right?'

Somehow the sound of his voice jolted her out of her catatonic state, and she could feel her tight muscles relaxing. What good would it do to put clothes on? They both knew what was going to happen later on. Why pretend otherwise?

She went to the door and opened it. He stood there, dressed in dark trousers and a soft white shirt. The cuffs were rolled up, the top button undone, and once again, Cara thought as she gazed at him, he had the advantage over her. She had expected him to appear in a brief robe or nightclothes, but now, fresh from the shower, the dark hair still a little damp, his face newly shaven, he looked as though he were ready to go out, while she stood there like a fool in her bathrobe.

His glance flicked over her briefly, but he made no comment. 'Shall we go in by the fire?' he said, and stood aside to let her precede him.

If he was disappointed she hadn't worn the gown he'd bought for her, he kept it to himself. He didn't speak at all as they walked noiselessly on the thick carpet through the hallway to the living room, and neither did she.

The fire was still crackling in the mammoth stone fireplace, and one dim lamp was burning near the wide couch that was placed squarely in front of it. As Cara sat down on the edge of one cushion, she saw that there were sandwiches, a large bowl of fresh fruit, several kinds of cheese and crackers, some smoked salmon and a dish of carrot curls and radish roses and tiny cherry tomatoes. There was a bottle of champagne in an ice-filled cooler, and soft music played from an obviously expensive stereo set in one corner of the room.

Quite a romantic setting, Cara thought, as she took in the seductive atmosphere she was certain he had deliberately created. All it needed was the gown he had bought to complete the picture. Clearly, she thought, Nicholas Curzon had a romantic streak. She almost laughed aloud at the irony of it. He wasn't satisfied merely to impose his will on her. No, his ego would demand her willing acquiescence.

It was then that the idea occurred to her. He had said he would tear up the bills of sale on the boats if she would marry him. Well, she had married him, hadn't she? Nothing had been said about her behaviour except that she was to do as she was told. If she did everything in her power to make life difficult for him, even while obeying him, perhaps he might be glad to get rid of her in a week or two. She found a miserable two weeks infinitely more acceptable than a lifetime of mindless servitude.

With this new hope, Cara began to relax, to feel more confident, less at a disadvantage. He obviously wanted something very badly that it was in her power to withhold, and it would give her great pleasure to deny him that satisfaction. If he wanted her, she was going to make him take her by force. It was her one weapon against him, and she intended to use it for all it was worth.

He was standing in front of the fire gazing down at her, and she looked calmly up at him. 'Where is Mrs Varga?' she asked in a conversational tone. She began to fill her plate.

He came to sit beside her. 'I imagine she's gone to bed,' he said shortly.

Cara smiled at the note of tension in his voice. It pleased her to see that in spite of all the advantages he held, he seemed ill-at-ease. She leaned back slightly on the cushions in a relaxed posture.

'She lives here, then?' she asked.

He gave her a narrow look. 'Yes. So does her husband. He takes care of the grounds and does odd jobs.'

'How nice for you,' she murmured. 'The gambling business must pay well for you to be able to afford servants, this house, your fancy car.' And me, she almost added.

He set his plate down then and gave her a long assessing look. She continued to pick at her food, barely tasting it. Then, to her surprise, he smiled.

'You're determined to think of me as some kind of shady character, aren't you, Cara?' His tone was pleasant. 'You do know, don't you, that gambling is legal in Nevada?'

'That doesn't make it right,' she retorted.

He raised his dark eyebrows. 'It does to me,' he said flatly. 'The casino has been in my family since nineteen-twenty-nine, the year gambling was legalised here. My grandfather started it. He was a silver miner who struck it rich, and the casino is only one of the Curzon family enterprises.'

She gave him an innocent look. 'Oh, I see. That makes it all right, then. What are these other enterprises? Prostitution? Drugs? Blackmail, certainly. You've proved how good you are at that.'

She watched with satisfaction as a dull, reddish flush spread across his face. 'I told you once, Cara,

that I'm a very patient man,' he said in a low
voice. 'But if you try hard enough, you'll succeed
in pushing me beyond even my limits.'

She lightly touched her napkin to her mouth, set
it down on the coffee table, and turned to give him
a direct gaze. The expression on his face was still
pleasant, but the mouth was pinched slightly, the
grey eyes faintly menacing.

'I'm not afraid of you, Nicholas,' she said
clearly.

His eyes gleamed. 'I'm glad to hear that,' he said
in a smooth tone. 'I want your co-operation, not
your terror.'

She laughed drily. 'Then you're in for a
disappointment because you won't get either from
me.'

In a flash his hand shot out and gripped her
arm. 'We'll see,' he said, and in one quick
movement, he was pushing her shoulders back on
the cushions of the couch, his upper body lying
heavily on top of her. She closed her eyes as the
dark head descended and felt his hard mouth
pressing on hers in a punishing, grinding kiss.

Her whole body stiffened automatically at his
touch, but this only seemed to inflame him further.
He was holding her head tightly between his hands
now, the warm mouth searching, his fingers
working their way up into the thick mass of her
dark hair. As he freed the pins holding it in place,
it fell heavily around her face. He pushed it aside
and was murmuring now in her ear.

'Ah, my lovely Cara. Relax. I won't hurt you.'
One hand went to her shoulder and slipped inside
the collar of her robe to trace the bony ridge
beneath her throat. 'You're so fragile, so delicate.'

With all her will, Cara fought down her revulsion at this sudden invasion of her privacy. She made her body go limp, her mind blank. She kept her arms still at her sides, her mouth clamped shut and sought frantically in her mind for some pretence, some imaginative vision that would blot out the reality of what was happening to her. She decided to pretend to herself that she was one of the early martyrs of the Church about to be ravaged by a Roman centurion, but when he lifted her up off the couch and started carrying her down the hall to the bedroom, she opened her eyes slightly to find him gazing down at her with a fiery glance. There was a determined set to the strong jaw, and the little self-deception fled from her mind at the sight of him.

'Don't think for a minute, Cara, that your possum act is going to stop me,' he said in a tight voice. 'I'm going to get full value for what I paid for, and, by God, before this night is over, you're going to enjoy it.'

She opened her eyes again. 'It will never happen,' she said steadily.

'We'll see.'

They were at her bedroom door now, and he reached out a hand to open it.

'No!' she cried. 'Not in there. You promised. That's my room.' She knew she'd have to go through with this travesty, but she didn't want him in her bed all night or have to see him there in the morning.

He hesitated a moment, then nodded. 'All right,' he said curtly, and strode across the hall to his own room.

He kicked the unlatched door open and went

inside the darkened room. When he came to the
wide bed, he set her down on top of it. She felt him
withdraw from her, and looked up at him through
half-closed eyes. He stood beside the bed staring
down at her and slowly unbuttoning his shirt. She
watched covertly as he slipped it off and threw it
on a nearby chair, and by the light that filtered
into the bedroom from the hall, she could see his
tanned upper body quite clearly.

At the sight of the broad shoulders and smooth
sinuous muscles of his arms and chest, something
strange began to stir in her, a disturbing warmth,
an unsettling ache. His chest and flat stomach
were lightly covered with fine silky hair that ended
and disappeared into the waistband of his dark
trousers. His hair, always so neatly combed, was
ruffled and one black lock fell across his forehead.
The hollows of his cheeks, his grey eyes, were
mysteriously shadowed, and the sudden thought
flashed into her mind that he was the most
beautiful man she had ever seen.

Slowly, he eased himself down on the bed beside
her. She couldn't take her eyes off him. She
watched, mesmerised, as he reached out to untie
her robe and spread it apart. He lifted her up in his
strong bare arms to pull it off her shoulders, and
suddenly she was ashamed of her old cotton
nightgown. He made no comment, however, as he
threw the robe aside and laid her head gently back
down on the pillows. His long fingers began to
unbutton the high neckline of her gown. She could
hear his heavy breathing in the stillness of the
room, and realised that it was her own breath she
heard as well as his.

It was then, for the first time, that she became

really frightened. No, she thought wildly, he's not beautiful. Inside he's ugly, a pirate, a blackmailer, a barbarian. She recalled fairy tales she had read as a child where it was fatal to look upon certain dangerous objects, and she knew that she had to fight against her own weakness.

With an effort, she snapped her eyes shut, but not before she saw his head come down towards her. Once again, with the sight of him and what he was doing to her blotted out, she could make her body go limp, and when his hot mouth settled firmly on hers, she kept her lips firmly closed.

'Put your arms around me, Cara,' he murmured. His mouth on hers opened wider and she could feel his tongue seeking, trying to force an entry.

Jerkily, she raised her arms and held them stiffly around his neck. She would obey, she thought grimly, but would never respond, and she would not open her mouth to him. Then she felt the bed give under him as he settled his long length against her. His hand slid slowly down over her throat and settled on her breast. She could feel the warmth of it through the worn material of her gown, and when it began to move, gently, lightly, over the hardening peak, she heard him give a low moan of pleasure.

Cara had never in her life experienced anything like the sensations that were beginning to stir through her now. His hand moved to her other breast, slipping inside the loosened neckline first to trace the soft bare fullness and then to brush over the taut nipple. His lips moved to her throat, and his other hand swept slowly down the length of her body, across her stomach, her thighs, then up under her nightgown, burning on her bare flesh.

Her mouth opened to him instinctively, and she felt his tongue slide inside and probe gently. She simply couldn't resist the tide of desire that had begun to sweep her along. But with the unmistakable desire came a sudden overpowering revulsion, not against the man who was working such magic on her responsive body, but against herself and her own primitive, mindless reactions.

Nausea began to gnaw at her stomach as it dawned on her what she was doing, and she stiffened, fighting it. She felt cold perspiration break out on her forehead, a choking sensation grip her by the throat, a clamminess over her whole body.

She tore herself away from him and rose up on her elbows, choking and gagging. Nicholas twisted sideways and switched on a lamp beside the bed. When he turned back to her, she covered her face in her hands.

'What the hell . . .' he muttered, and began to pull her hands away from her face.

She gave him one agonised look. 'I—I—' she gasped, turning away from him and trying to take in deep gulps of air to quiet her churning stomach.

Then, with a loud groan, she flung herself off the bed. She looked wildly around, saw the open door of the adjoining bathroom and stumbled inside. She just made it to the basin, retching and heaving, and when it was over, she leaned limply up against the counter, her forehead pressed against the cool mirror, drained and empty, trembling from head to foot.

Finally, still shaking, she opened her eyes and turned the water on in the basin. She cleaned it as best she could in the dim light, then scooped up a

handful of water and rinsed out her mouth. Her
legs felt like rubber under her and she had to
clutch the edge of the counter to keep from
falling.

Suddenly, the overhead light was turned on. She
straightened up, turned, and saw Nicholas leaning
in the doorway. His arms were crossed in front of
his bare chest, and he was glaring at her, a look of
cold fury in the grey eyes.

'That was quite a performance,' he snapped.
'But if you think . . .'

'Performance!' she cried weakly. 'How can you. . .'

'But if you think,' he ground on as though she
hadn't spoken, 'that I'm impressed with this
display of outraged virtue, you're sadly mistaken.'

She could only stare at him. Hostility emanated
from him in palpable waves, but as she looked
more closely, she could see something else in the
forbidding expression. It was hurt, she realised.
She had wounded him with that sudden attack of
nausea in his arms. He obviously thought her
wretched illness was a reaction against his
lovemaking. This realisation gave her the strength
she needed. She turned from him, features
composed, and reached out to turn on the water
again. Slowly, methodically, she finished cleaning
the basin, then turned the water off and began to
walk towards him.

'There is no way I could have manufactured
what happened,' she said. 'If you had any sense,
you'd realise that.' She smiled coolly. 'But then, if
you had any sense, you never would have forced
me into this marriage in the first place. You've got
the wife you wanted so badly, and I didn't lift a
finger to stop you from exercising your rights. But

nothing in our agreement said that I had to like it. I can't help it if your touch revolts me. Now, will you let me pass? I'm tired. It's been a long day, and I still feel queasy. Or do you want to make me sick again tonight?'

She knew he was so angry by now that there was a real danger he might actually strike her. His hands were balled up into fists, his arms held rigid at his sides. She didn't care. Let him hit her. She gazed up at him with a defiant look.

Suddenly, the tension seemed to ease out of him, and a mocking smile twisted on the firm line of his mouth. He stepped aside to let her pass.

'All right, Cara,' he said in a low menacing tone, 'Have it your way. But if you have any ideas about leaving here or that I'll send you away, get rid of them. I still hold those bills of sale, and make no mistake, I'll exercise them if I have to.'

Her eyes widened. 'You said you'd tear them up,' she whispered.

The cruel smile broadened. 'I lied,' he said casually. 'What else did you expect from a gambler?'

'You're despicable,' she spat at him.

'And you're a very poor actress.' The grey eyes narrowed. 'Do you think I wasn't aware of your response to me back there?' He gestured with his dark head to the bed behind him. 'Did you think I wouldn't notice how your mouth softened and opened to me?' His voice was low and rhythmic now. 'Or how those lovely breasts swelled and hardened under my hands?' He shook his head slowly, still smiling. 'A man knows when a woman is ready for him. Believe me, Cara. You can't hide it.' The smile was triumphant now.

The cruel words were a hundred times more humiliating than the blow she had been expecting. 'I hated you before,' she choked out at last in a low voice. 'So much that I didn't think it was possible for you to sink any lower in my estimation. But you just did.'

With that, she sailed past him, her head held high. She grabbed her robe off the bed where he had tossed it earlier and walked out of the room, his mocking laughter following her until she was in her own bedroom, and the door firmly shut behind her.

CHAPTER FOUR

THE next morning Cara stood at the window of her bedroom gazing out at the most beautiful sight she had ever seen. Stretching just beyond the sloping grounds of the house was the clear bright blue of Lake Tahoe, the snow-covered Sierra Nevadas encircling it like a sapphire in a ring of diamonds. Even at this distance, surely more than a hundred yards, she could see the rocky bottom of the clean, sparkling water.

There were several varieties of pine, fir, spruce and hemlock that she recognised dotting the jutting promontories of land that curved around the lake and screened the opulent houses built along the shore. The sun shone brightly down on the reddening aspen and birch trees, harbingers of the imminent fall.

So entranced was she by the stunning vista spread out before her that she could momentarily forget Nicholas Curzon, forget that she was bound to a man she loathed, and forget, especially, the sheer overwhelming power of the physical response he had evoked in her last night when she lay in his arms. But not for long. In spite of the beauty and luxury of her new home, the dull ache in her heart lingered to spoil it all.

She turned away from the window and went into the bathroom. She had already showered, washed her hair, unpacked and dressed in her old grey skirt and green sweater, and now her empty stomach began to protest with the first stirrings of real hunger she had felt in days.

During the night, in the aftermath of her sudden wretched sickness, she had thought long and hard about her situation. It was quite clear to her that the revulsion and nausea she had experienced in Nicholas Curzon's bed were far more a reaction against her own body's treacherous response to his skilful lovemaking than against the man himself. But he must never know that, she thought firmly as she combed out her long black hair in front of the mirror, and somehow she must school herself so that it would never happen again. Her one hope was that he would send her away, tire of her, or become so sick of her passive resistance to him that he'd be glad to tear up the notes just to be rid of her.

Slowly, she pinned her still damp hair back in its knot. He could easily have taken her last night, she thought. She hadn't fought him. He must have known that. Yet he had deliberately, persistently held himself in check, moved slowly with her, simply in order to make her respond. And she had fallen into the trap, betrayed by a sensuality she never knew dwelled within her. It wasn't Nicholas Curzon who was her enemy, she realised now, but her own body, and she was determined to find a way to fight it.

She stepped out of her bedroom and glanced warily across the hall. Nicholas's door was open, the wide bed neatly made, and there was no sign of life. As she walked towards the front of the house, she could hear a radio playing somewhere in the distance. She made her way in that direction, past the spotless living room where they'd had supper the night before, until finally she came to the kitchen.

It was a bright, sunny room, painted a pale yellow, with cheerful sprigged muslin curtains at the window. Mrs Varga was standing with her back to her, busy at the counter and humming under her breath along with the music coming from a small radio. There was a bunch of yellow chrysanthemums on the round birch table in the corner by the windows, and the room smelled of spicy baking, warm and pleasant.

'Mrs Varga,' Cara said quietly.

The tall, grey-haired woman whirled around. 'Oh, Mrs Curzon,' she said. 'You startled me.'

'I'm sorry,' Cara apologised and walked into the room. 'I thought I'd see if I could find some breakfast. I know it's late. I don't want to disturb you.'

Mrs Varga had rinsed her hands and was drying them now on her apron. 'Not at all. Why don't you sit down at the table, and I'll fix you something.' She bustled about the kitchen, getting juice from the refrigerator and laying a place at the table. 'Mr Curzon likes a big breakfast,' she rambled on pleasantly, 'always the same thing. But you'll have to tell me what you like.'

Cara sat down at the table. The woman apparently intended to wait on her, and she might as well get used to it. She wouldn't welcome interference in her kitchen from her employer's new wife.

'Juice, coffee and toast will be fine,' she said. She glanced at the clock on the wall above the refrigerator. It was past ten o'clock. 'I'm not usually such a late riser, but yesterday was rather hectic, and I slept in this morning.' She paused, watching as Mrs Varga plugged in a fresh pot of coffee. 'Has Nicholas—Mr Curzon—already left?'

'Oh, my yes. He's an early riser. Likes to get to his office by eight o'clock, and it's a good thirty-mile drive into Reno.'

'Office?' Cara enquired faintly. 'I thought . . . That is, what about the casino?'

Mrs Varga stopped and stared at her. 'Oh, Mr Logan manages the casino. Has for years. Mr Curzon never sets foot in it if he doesn't have to. He has enough on his hands running Curzon Enterprises since his father died.'

'Yes,' Cara murmured, sipping her juice. 'Of course. Will he . . . That is, does he come home for lunch?'

'Oh, goodness, no,' Mrs Varga said, setting down a steaming fragrant cup of coffee and a plate of fresh buttered toast before her. 'He's lucky to make it in time for dinner most nights, and sometimes he stays at the apartment in town all night.' She broke off suddenly. Her eyes widened, and she clapped a hand over her mouth. Flushing deeply, she turned away and began fussily clearing the counter. 'Of course, that was before he was married,' she muttered.

Cara had to laugh. 'Of course,' she agreed. 'Don't worry about it, please, Mrs Varga. I'm not the jealous type.' Far from it where he's concerned, she thought drily as she spread honey on her toast.

Mrs Varga turned and smiled sheepishly. 'No,' she said, a glint of appreciation in her eye, 'and if you don't mind my saying so, I'm sure there's no need where you're concerned. You must know that lots of women have tried to pin him down, and I'm not saying he's been a saint, but you're the first that ever made him even think of settling down, and I can see why.' She reddened again. 'I know I talk too much,' she mumbled. 'It's just that I want to see him happy, and I can tell by the way he looks at you that you're the one that can do it. He's a good man.'

'Thank you, Mrs Varga,' Cara said politely. 'You're very kind.' If the woman only knew, she thought, that this 'good' man had virtually won her in a poker game, and that far from having any desire to make him happy, her one goal was to get as far away from him as possible.

After breakfast, Cara put on her heavy jacket and went outside to explore the grounds of her new home. Hopefully, her temporary home, she thought as she walked down the curving brick path towards the lake.

There was a decided chill in the air. She tied a woollen scarf over her head and shoved her hands into the pockets of her jacket. At the water's edge was a long planked dock with a small boathouse built at the end of it. She walked towards it now, and stopped halfway to lean over the wooden railing and gaze down into the transparent blue water.

Suddenly, she thought of her family. She wondered how her mother was doing without her. Before they left, Nicholas had arranged with a local visiting nurse service to send in someone to care for her, but Cara knew it wouldn't be the same. She missed her mother, and wanted to care for her herself, but when Nicholas had suggested moving her to the hospital in Reno, Cara had emphatically declined. Since her main objective was to get out of here one way or another, there was no point in disturbing her mother by moving her away from home.

Her brooding thoughts were interrupted by the sound of Mrs Varga calling her name. She turned and saw her at the top of the brick path near the house, waving at her frantically.

'Telephone, Mrs Curzon,' she shouted.

Cara ran quickly up the path. Maybe it was her family calling. A cold tremor of fear gripped her. Was her mother worse? As she approched the house, however, she slowed her steps when she saw the broad smile on Mrs Varga's face.

'It's Mr Curzon,' she announced, obviously pleased. 'You can take it in the living room if you like.'

'Thank you,' Cara said. She went through the kitchen to the living room and picked up the telephone. 'Yes,' she said coolly.

There was a short silence. Then, 'Such enthusiasm is overwhelming,' Nicholas commented drily. 'Especially in a new bride.'

'What do you want?' she asked in the same flat tone.

'I don't think I dare tell you what I want over the telephone.' The deep voice was low and suggestive. Cara bit her tongue to hold back a sharp retort and waited silently.

When he spoke again, his voice was brisk and businesslike. 'Word has got out of our marriage,' he said, 'and we're invited to a party tonight in our honour.'

'I see,' she replied.

He waited, but when she didn't make any comment, he went on. 'Well?' he said curtly. 'What do you think?'

'What difference does it make what I think?' she asked. An edge of anger had crept into her voice. He was the one giving all the orders. Did he expect her to dance for joy at the prospect of going to one of his silly parties? 'Just tell me what you want me to do.'

There was another silence. 'Very well,' he said at last. 'I will. I want you to go to the party with me and make a heroic effort to enjoy yourself.'

She laughed shortly. 'Yes, sir. Anything else?'

She could hear him draw in his breath. 'You're determined to make this as difficult as possible for both of us, aren't you, Cara?'

'What did you expect?' she said through clenched teeth. 'You make all the rules. What more do you want?'

'I want you to quit fighting me,' he said. 'I want you to start acting like my wife instead of a sulky child.'

'Then you're asking too much. My feelings and thoughts are my own. They weren't included in the agreement. I don't even like you, Nicholas. How can you expect me to act like a wife?'

'All right, Cara, have it your way,' he said wearily. 'Do you have anything to wear to the party? There's a car in the garage you can use if you want to come into Reno to do some shopping.'

'No, thank you,' she replied politely. 'I have my wedding dress.'

He laughed. 'Ah, yes, your funeral weeds.'

'Why not? It's the way I feel.'

'Then you'll just have to suffer, won't you?' he said silkily. 'It's your choice. I'll be home early. We're invited for dinner, so be ready to leave at six o'clock.'

He hung up then. Cara slowly replaced the receiver. A party, she thought bitterly. Just about the last thing she wanted. She shivered a little at the thought of what Nicholas Curzon's friends would be like. It didn't matter what she wore or how she looked and behaved. She could never fit into his world or feel comfortable with the kind of people in it.

But she turned out to be wrong on every count. Not only were the people she met that evening pleasant and friendly and genuinely welcoming to her as Nicholas's wife, but no one gave her severe black dress and plain hairstyle a second glance. In fact, of the twenty women at the party, every conceivable variation in style could be seen, from a mannish tweed trousersuit to an extremely revealing, low-cut cocktail dress.

The party was held at the home of a college professor who taught at the University of Nevada in Reno. The house was a modest one, set on a quiet street half a mile away from the more expensive lakefront property, and although it was far roomier than her family's cottage at Southport, it didn't compare with the rich opulence of Nicholas's home.

A simple buffet supper was laid out on a long table in the dining room, and they ate at smaller tables which had been set up in a circular pattern around the walls of the connecting living room. It was a noisy group. They all seemed to know each

other quite well, and there was a great deal of loud
chatter over the music coming from a hidden tape
deck.

Cara and Nicholas sat at a table with their host
and hostess, Robert and Diana Hathaway, a
pleasant middle-aged couple who seemed to be
old, intimate friends of Nicholas.

'Well, Nick,' Robert Hathaway boomed loudly
when they had filled their plates and sat down to
eat. 'I never thought I'd see the day.' He was a
large heavyset man with a very red face and shiny
bald head. Bright blue eyes beamed appreciatively
now at Cara. 'We were all convinced our Nick was
a confirmed bachelor,' he explained, 'but I can see
now why he waited so long. All this time he had
you hidden away up in the wilds of Washington.'
He gave Nicholas a sly look. 'Clever devil.'

Cara had to smile, even though his highly vocal
comments made her decidedly uncomfortable. If
he only knew, she thought as she lowered her eyes
and pushed her food around on her plate.

'Don't mind him,' Diana Hathaway said
comfortably. She was a plump motherly type with
disorderly grey hair. 'He just says whatever comes
into his head. Loudly, I might add. It comes from
bossing his students around.' She turned to her
husband with a frown. 'Can't you see you're
embarrassing Cara, you idiot?'

'No, of course not,' Cara murmured, giving
Robert a reassuring smile. 'It's perfectly all right.'

'Well, I for one,' Diana went on, 'would like to
hear the sound of someone else's voice for a
change.' She gave her husband a withering look,
but he only grinned broadly and continued tucking
the food away. Diana turned to Cara. 'We're all

dying to learn more about you. Is it true you've known Nick for ten years?'

Cara almost choked on her food at that. 'Well, in a manner of speaking, I suppose you could say that. It wasn't until—uh—quite recently that we knew each other well.'

She told her then about her life at the village by the ocean, the charter service run by her father and brothers, but omitted any mention of the gambling debt and the peculiar way her new husband had chosen to collect on it.

Through her whole recitation, she could see Nicholas out of the corner of her eye lounging back in his chair, chewing thoughtfully, listening to her every word. He seemed totally at ease, but then, she thought, he would be. These are his friends, his territory. I'm the stranger, the one who has to prove herself.

'Well,' Diana said when Cara had finished, 'I still think it's terribly romantic. Just think, to only see each other once a year and then to suddenly fall in love and get married. Just like that.' She turned to Nicholas with an appreciative grin.

'Yes,' he said easily. 'Just like that.' He glanced across the table at Cara and gave her a secret smile.

After dinner, the card tables were cleared away and Cara and Nicholas were ensconced on the couch so that people could come to them in turn and offer their congratulations and be introduced to Cara. As she smiled politely at each in turn and spoke the trite platitudes to them, she felt like a faker. She hated the lie she was living, hated having to pretend she was a real bride, hated listening to all the sly comments about Nicholas's successful evasion of marriage before she came along. He, on the other hand, seemed to be perfectly comfortable with the situation that was so awkward for her, even to be enjoying it.

The last person to approach them was a beautiful blonde, heavily tanned and dressed in a skin-tight, low-cut white dress that left absolutely nothing to the imagination when she leaned over to put her hands on Nicholas's shoulders and plant a firm kiss on his mouth.

'Ah, Nick,' she said huskily with a playful smile on the full painted lips, 'you've broken my heart.'

She gave Cara a cool glance, as if to say, 'You've got him now, but watch out for me.' Cara returned the smile. She wanted to retort that the woman was welcome to him, but instead sat quietly with her hands folded in her lap, waiting for Nicholas to introduce her.

'Cara,' he said, turning to her, 'this is Moira Faraday, an old friend.'

The blonde laughed, a silvery tinkling sound. 'A *very* old friend,' she said. She put a perfectly manicured hand on his cheek. 'We grew up together.' She blinked bright blue eyes. 'Just like brother and sister.'

A few couples had drifted out to the middle of the living-room floor where the rug had been rolled up for dancing. Nicholas turned to Cara.

'Would you care to dance, Mrs Curzon?' he murmured.

'No thank you,' she said politely. Cara didn't even know how to dance, but she wasn't going to tell him that. She glanced up at Moira Faraday. 'But you go ahead if you like.'

Moira's finely pencilled eyebrows raised slightly

at that, and she gave Cara a calculating look. 'How generous,' she said softly, then turned to Nicholas and held out a hand. 'Come on, darling. Your bride has given her permission.'

'Nicholas doesn't need my permission to do anything,' Cara said calmly. 'He knows I'm not in the least jealous.'

He shot her a dark look and shifted in his chair slightly as though to rise, but then, before he was halfway out of the chair, he settled back down again. Slowly and deliberately he reached over and took one of Cara's hands. Still holding her gaze steadily, he clasped the hand firmly between both of his own. Then he looked up at Moira.

'I'm on my honeymoon, Moira,' he said easily. 'I think I'll stay with my wife.'

Moira straightened up and stood looking down at them. 'Of course,' she said at last. 'I understand. But when the honeymoon is over, you know where to find me.'

Nicholas started to laugh. With one last brilliant smile, Moira turned and walked away. Still chuckling, he turned to Cara.

'You mustn't mind Moira,' he said. 'She's a spoiled rich girl who makes a career out of shocking people.'

'I don't mind her in the least,' Cara replied. She did wonder, however, whether they had ever been lovers, and the thought made her vaguely uncomfortable.

Nicholas was still holding her hand, and now he began to move his fingers lightly back and forth over the inside of her wrist. She didn't at all like the way the gentle pressure made her feel, and she started to pull her hand away. But his hold on it tightened immediately and he linked his fingers through hers.

'Relax,' he said, bending towards her. His lips just barely grazed her cheek. 'Surely you don't mind pretending just for a little while that you enjoy my touch.'

'I'll do my best,' she retorted with a fake smile, 'but I never was a very good actress.'

For the next few hours they sat together on the sidelines, watching the dancers and talking to the other guests. Nicholas never once left her side, and as the evening progressed, Cara was surprised at how comfortable she felt with these people. They all seemed to be genuinely fond of Nicholas and made a special effort to include her as his wife, as though sensing her natural shyness and reserve. While they all spoke warmly to her, no one pushed.

Finally, at eleven o'clock, Nicholas stood up. Still holding her hand, he looked down at her. 'You're tired,' he said in a low voice. 'I think it's time we went home.'

There was an intense, brooding expression on his face that made Cara shrink inwardly. Distracted by the friendly crowd of people, she had forgotten all about last night, and now she realised that what Nicholas had on his mind was a repetition of it. He wasn't the kind to give up easily.

They said their good nights and went outside. It was cold out, a bright moon shining in the black sky, and Nicholas held her closely to his side as they walked towards the car. It was only a short distance to his house, and in the darkness of the car, she watched him covertly out of the corner of her eye while he drove.

After this evening with his friends, she was even more puzzled by his motive in marrying her. Here was a man who seemed to have everything. Money, position, good friends who obviously respected him, genuinely cared for him. A beautiful, desirable woman who appeared to be bent on getting him into her bed, married or not. Good looks, she had to admit, gazing at him now.

His fine, strong profile was silhouetted against the street lights on the narrow main road that curved around the lake. He was by far the best-looking man there tonight. He carried himself well, with an air of authority and confidence that never quite spilled over into arrogance. She couldn't for the life of her fathom what he wanted with her, why he had gone to such lengths to force her to marry him when they both knew he could have had her as his mistress for as long as he chose. Was it possible her mother was right? That, wanting her, he had done the honourable thing? No, she decided, an honourable man would not have forced himself on her in the first place.

She jumped a little at the sound of his voice when he spoke. 'Well,' he said, as they turned into the drive that wound up to the house, 'what did you think?'

'About what?' she asked.

He pulled up in front of the house, shut off the engine and turned to her. 'About my friends,' he said.

'They were quite nice,' she said primly, hating to admit it, but knowing it was true.

He raised one dark eyebrow and smiled broadly. 'See any suspicious characters? Gangsters?'

He seemed to be laughing at her. This made her

angry, on top of the dread that was building slowly inside her at what lay ahead tonight. Without answering him, she turned and opened her door. By the time she had got out and had started walking towards the house, he had moved swiftly around the car to walk beside her and was ahead of her now, unlocking the front door.

Once inside, she started immediately towards her room, but he pushed the door shut behind him and reached for her, holding her back by her arm.

'Would you like a nightcap?' he asked from behind her.

'No, thank you. I'm tired. I'd like to go to bed.' She'd had a few glasses of wine at the party, and they had made her sleepy.

'Let's go then,' he said, and she stiffened as she felt his arms come around her and lift her up. He started walking with her down the hall, past her bedroom to his own.

He set her down inside, closed the door and flicked on the wall switch that turned on a dim lamp by the side of the wide bed. She stood rigid and unmoving, watching as he took off his jacket, then his tie. He tossed them on a chair and turned to her. Slowly, his eyes never leaving hers, he walked towards her until he stood only inches away, looking down at her with gleaming hooded grey eyes. He didn't utter a word, but the expression on his face spoke volumes.

Finally, the tension became unbearable. 'Why, Nicholas?' she whispered. 'Why are you doing this?'

He smiled and put a hand out to cup her chin. She shuddered at his touch. 'You're my wife,' he said.

'But why me? Why not Moira? She wants you. I don't.'

His expression hardened at that. 'Because I don't want Moira. I want you.'

She twisted her head away. 'In other words, you just want what you can't have,' she said harshly.

He forced her head back with his strong grip. 'Oh, but I *can* have you,' he said smoothly. 'I *do* have what I want.'

'Yes,' she said bitterly. 'Bought and paid for.'

He only smiled again and bent his dark head until his mouth met hers, brushing against it lightly, the tip of his tongue outlining her soft lips. Cara closed her eyes. He was playing with her now, drawing her underlip into his mouth, pulling at it, then moving his lips to her cheek, her jawline, the lobe of her ear.

'Turn around,' he murmured. She obeyed, slowly, mechanically, and felt his hands move to her shoulders, the back of her neck. There was a rasping sound as he unzipped her dress, and she stood shivering as he slid it off her shoulders and let it fall in a heap about her feet.

His hands were at her waist now, sliding back and forth over the silky material of her black slip. With all her strength she tried to blot out the sensations that assailed her, to fight down the warm tide that began to flow through her, but when the strong hands glided slowly upward to cup her breasts, she gasped aloud at the touch.

He pulled her back against his chest, his hands caressing, kneading the soft fullness, and then he slid the straps of her slip off her shoulders so that it settled around her waist loosely.

He turned her around then to face him. She

couldn't look at him, but she sensed his gaze boring into her. He reached around to unclasp the back closing of her bra, then it, too, was removed. She felt him withdraw from her, and after a moment she opened her eyes slightly to see him staring at her bare breasts, the hunger in his eyes unmistakable.

'My lovely Cara,' he breathed. 'So beautiful. Watching you sitting there all evening tonight, so prim and proper in your black dress, so remote and cool, I could hardly keep my hands off you.'

He reached out a hand and placed it gently over one breast. At the strong warm touch, an overwhelming sensation of heat flooded through her. She closed her eyes and bit her lip to fight back the insidious tide, but when his fingers began rubbing over the throbbing peak of her breast, it was all she could do not to moan aloud at the sheer pleasure washing over her, filling her whole body.

'You see,' he was murmuring now as his fingers slid to her other breast and began to work their magic there. 'You do want me.'

His arms came around her then, crushing her to him, and his open mouth descended on hers, his tongue probing past the lips that seemed to open automatically to him. His hands slid down over her bare back, underneath the slip at her waist and clutched her hips, pulling her lower body up against his so that the hard thrust of his arousal was unmistakable.

Every instinct of Cara's being shouted at her to let go, to respond, to yield to the fire raging within her. She longed to feel his bare chest against her breasts, to run her own hands over the hard-

muscled body, so different from her own, so
strange and compelling. She wanted to explore
him as she would an alien land that contained rich
delights she could only guess at in her inexperi-
ence.

Then, just as she was about to abandon her
resistance and fling her arms around his neck, the
familiar nausea began to gnaw at the pit of her
stomach. She tried to fight it down, but once again
a clammy perspiration began to break out over her
whole body, and a bitterness rose in her throat.

With a violent jerk of her head, she twisted
away from him, panting and gagging. He pulled
back, startled, his hands still at her waist, and
gazed down at her.

'Cara, what is it?'

She couldn't look at him. She was ashamed of
the illness she couldn't control, but still, with its
advent had come a breath of sanity. She didn't
want to respond to him, she thought wildly as she
choked back the nausea. Why, then, did he have
this power over her?

'I can't,' she muttered. 'I just can't.' She looked
up at him bleakly.

He searched her waxen face carefully in a
penetrating examination. The concern that had been
in his eyes before was gone now, and they had
narrowed into slits. His mouth was set in a firm
line, and he dropped his hands from her waist with
a sigh of frustration. He stepped back from her
and ran a hand over his dark head in a gesture of
defeat.

'What is it with you?' he ground out between
clenched teeth. 'What is there about me that does
this to you?'

She bit her lip and closed her eyes, her stomach still churning. 'I can't help it, Nicholas.'

'God, don't you think I know that?' His glance fell on her still bare breasts, and he grimaced as if he were in pain. Then he reached out and pulled the black slip up to cover her nakedness, sliding the straps back over her shoulders. 'All right, Cara,' he said in a hopeless tone. 'I can see it's no use. I won't push it any more. But, damn it, I know you want me as much as I want you.'

'I don't know what I want,' she said in a low voice and looked away. She had to get out of there, away from his disturbing presence. She wanted to be alone, to think, to try to sort out the conflicting emotions raging within her.

'Go on, then,' he said gruffly. 'Go to bed. Alone. Live like a nun if that's what you want. I won't bother you again. There's just so much of this I can take. I've never had to force a woman yet, and I'm not going to start now. When you're ready to admit to your real feelings, you come to me.'

Cara stumbled out of the room and crossed the hall to her own bedroom. Somehow she got herself undressed and ready for bed, but it wasn't until she was lying there in the dark, motionless, gazing up at the ceiling, that it dawned on her that the nausea had passed. What's more, it hadn't been as severe this time. She never had become actually ill, as she had last night.

Thank God for that, she thought, then immediately caught herself. Her eyes widened in the darkness. What am I saying? Why should I be glad that I'm beginning to be able to respond to that hateful man? How can I even think such a thing after what he's done?

Then she remembered how his mouth had tasted on hers, how his hands had felt on her breast, and the lean hardness of his body pressed against hers. She remembered, too, the rare moments when she was able to forget hostility to him and could recognise and appreciate the sheer beauty and appeal of the man.

'Oh, God,' she whispered aloud. 'What's happening to me?' She didn't know what to think, what she wanted, even what she *should* be thinking and wanting. Wasn't he her enemy? But why, then, was she so drawn to him physically?

All her life, she had walked a straight path, knowing what she wanted, and, when it turned out she couldn't have it, calmly doing what her sense of duty and responsibility told her to do. She had suffered, but in her sheltered, limited experience, the right way was always unmistakably clear. Now, for the first time in her life, she had fallen prey to an insidious confusion, a weak self-doubt, and she didn't know how to handle it.

Tossing and turning through the long night, she tried to penetrate the mystery of her own warring emotions. Finally, exhausted, she found one salient fact to hang on to. Nicholas had said he would leave her alone from now on, that she would have to come to him if she wanted him. Didn't that one fact resolve the conflict? Never in a million years would she do that, she vowed, and with that certainty to hang on to, she finally calmed herself and slept at last.

CHAPTER FIVE

'I'D like to go to church,' Cara said to Mrs Varga the next day. 'Is there one up here at the lake, or will I have to go into Reno?'

She had risen late again, and had made up her mind while she showered and dressed that as long as she was stuck here, she might as well try to make some kind of normal life for herself.

It turned out that there was indeed a tiny chapel at the far end of the lake on the California side, which Mrs Varga herself attended. A priest from the larger church in Carson City drove up each Sunday morning to say Mass, and since today was Saturday, they arranged to go together in the morning.

Nicholas had been gone again when she had finally got up. Apparently, his working hours extended even into the weekend. Or perhaps, she thought, as she walked down to the lake after breakfast, he just wanted to get away from her.

She leaned on the wooden railing along the boat dock and stared unseeing down into the crystal blue water of the lake. There were large stones at the bottom, smooth and covered with a soft, greenish moss. A school of tiny fish appeared suddenly in a flurry of motion, darted about, then vanished.

It was very beautiful, Cara thought, the weather cold and clear, the scenery magnificent. But it wasn't the ocean. She thought with longing of her small village, the pounding surf and rolling tides of the constantly changing sea, the long stretches of deserted rocky beach where she could walk for hours, alone with her thoughts, safe in a familiar private world of her own.

She thought of the rough fishermen and their families, silent, hard-working people who had known her from childhood, of her family who, with all their faults, loved her and accepted her—*needed* her—just as she was. A wave of homesickness washed over her, almost taking her breath away in its painful intensity.

She simply wasn't cut out to be a rich man's plaything, she thought sadly. She turned, leaned back against the railing and glanced up the broad grassy slope towards the house. All this luxury, the beautiful home, opulent furnishings, the cars, the money, all were nothing compared to her family and that feeling of belonging. She fought back tears, determined not to give in to the self-pity, and started walking slowly back to the house.

There was a large spreading maple tree not far from the house, with a wooden bench underneath. The ground was strewn with yellow leaves which crunched underfoot as she made her way towards the tree. She sat down and propped her chin in her hands, pondering her situation and what she could do to make it more tolerable.

She'd have to find something to do with herself, she decided finally. It looked as though she was trapped here. Even though her violent reaction to Nicholas's lovemaking must be a terrible disappointment to him, to say the least, he still seemed determined to keep her with him. God only knows why, she thought, but a bargain is a bargain, and he owns me now.

She got up and went into the house through the kitchen door. Mrs Varga had left a large pot of fragrant soup simmering on the stove, and the room was warm and cosy after the chilly outdoors. Cara took off her heavy jacket and ladled out a bowl of soup for her lunch. It was after one o'clock, and she'd only had her usual light breakfast.

She sat down at the kitchen table and started to eat, still brooding. He had said last night he'd leave her alone from now on. She had hurt him, she knew, by the nausea she couldn't choke down whenever he made love to her. Perhaps eventually his wounded pride would convince him to let her go. In the meantime, she couldn't just cower in this big house all by herself. There was nothing for her to do. Mrs Varga took care of running the house and wouldn't welcome interference. She'd just have to try, anyway, to find some kind of useful occupation.

She finally decided she would broach the subject with Nicholas that night at dinner. Late that afternoon she set the table in the living room in front of the fire, thinking that perhaps the cosy atmosphere would make him more approachable. Mrs Varga had put a casserole in the oven and made a salad before she left to go home to the apartment over the garage where she lived with her husband.

It was after six when Nicholas came home from wherever it was he spent his days. Cara was in the kitchen tossing the salad and getting rolls ready to put in the oven when she heard the car pull up in front of the house, his step on the front porch. She listened as he came inside, then heard him go down the hall to his bedroom, and in a few minutes, the sound of his shower running.

As soon as it stopped, she set the rolls in the oven and began dishing up their plates. She put on a pot of coffee while the rolls heated, then stood in the middle of the room, hesitating, suddenly unsure of herself. It dawned on her that she knew nothing about his habits. Maybe he was a late diner. Maybe he preferred to eat more formally in the dining room.

Finally, she shrugged and made up her mind to just go ahead with her plans. If he didn't like it, she had no doubt he wouldn't hesitate to let her know it. She put the plates on a tray and carried it into the living room. He was sitting in front of the fire and glanced up at her now as she came into the room.

'Would you like a drink?' he asked.

His tone was polite, distant. She stood at the doorway and gazed at him. He was dressed casually in dark trousers and a heavy white turtleneck sweater, lounging comfortably on the wide couch, the daily newspaper spread out on the coffee table before him, a drink in his hand. Why did the sight of him unsettle her so? she wondered.

'No,' she replied, walking stiffly towards him. 'No, thank you.' She hesitated. 'I dished up dinner. Mrs Varga left a casserole. Maybe you're not ready to eat.'

'I'm ready,' he said briefly. He downed the last of his drink and cleared the paper off the table.

She set the plates down and sat beside him.

They ate in silence for a while. Finally, she turned to him.

'I'd like to talk to you,' she said.

He was bending over the table, eating, and merely gave her a sideways glance without speaking. The fire crackled loudly, and outside a wind had come up. Otherwise the room was quite still. Cara had the uneasy feeling that they were the only two people in the universe. She took a deep breath.

'Am I to understand,' she plunged on, 'that you still intend to keep me here, to go on with this marriage, even though . . .' She faltered.

He turned, then, and gave her a cool stare, the dark eyes expressionless. 'Even though my love-making sickens you?' he asked easily.

Cara reddened and looked down at her plate. 'That's putting it rather bluntly,' she murmured.

He set his fork down and leaned back on the couch, one long arm spread over the back of it. 'I see no point in skirting unpleasant truths,' he went on. 'It's a simple fact that whenever I come near you, you turn green and start gagging.'

She gave him a quick look. Even though his tone was controlled and matter-of-fact, she could sense the underlying bitterness in his admission that his impressive masculine charm had no effect on her except to turn her stomach. She was aware that this wasn't quite accurate, that her reaction was not entirely against him, but she wasn't willing to face the implications of that truth within herself, much less discuss it with him.

'I've tried,' she said in a low voice. 'I haven't fought you. I had every intention of honouring our agreement.'

'I know that,' he said evenly.

She would have given a great deal at that moment to see into his mind, his heart. What was he thinking and feeling? Surely his male pride had been badly wounded? Yet he seemed to accept it, even to be unconcerned. That could only mean one thing. She turned to him.

'Then, you'll let me leave?' She tried to keep the eagerness out of her voice, afraid of angering him and destroying the dim ray of hope.

'No,' he replied flatly. 'I will not.' Her face fell, but he went on. 'I told you I wanted a wife, and that I wanted you. For more reasons than sex, to put it crudely. That's easy enough to find if I want it.'

She believed him. His glamorous friend, Moira, had made that only too clear last night. She watched him now as he bent over his dinner again, trying to fathom what his motives were, why he was so determined to keep her as his wife when it must be clear to him by now that it would never be a real marriage.

'What about children?' she asked at last.

He stopped with his fork halfway to his mouth, set it down, and turned to give her an odd look. 'What about them?'

'Don't you want children?'

'Yes. Of course I do. Don't you?'

She looked away and stared into the flickering fire. 'I don't know. I've never thought about it. I never even intended to marry.' She paused for a moment, then said, 'If you want children, why don't you let me go and find someone who will give them to you?'

'I told you,' he said patiently. 'I want you. There are worse things than a childless marriage. Be-

sides . . .' He broke off, frowning, as though he had
said more than he intended, and turned back to
his dinner.

Besides what? Cara wondered. What had he
been about to say and then changed his mind? She
pondered this while they finished their dinner in
silence, but it wasn't until she had carried their
plates into the kitchen and was pouring out the
coffee that it came to her.

Of course, she thought, pausing with the pot in
midair. He'd said it himself last night, that he
would leave her alone until she came to him. He
was counting on her eventual surrender to his
irresistible charms!

She set the coffee pot down hard on the burner
and leaned up against the stove. Her mind raced.
It will never happen, she vowed. Even last night,
choking and gagging, she would have gone
through with it. It was what she had agreed to. But
go to him willingly? Never! He could wait until
doomsday.

Now that she had a better understanding of
where matters stood between them and what was
probably going on in this strange man's head, her
confidence began to return to her. All she had to
do was wait him out. He wasn't going to force the
issue. He was confident he'd win in the end. She
reached for the coffee pot again and finished filling
the cups. He would have a long wait, she thought
grimly. She would never forgive him for what he'd
done. He'd find out eventually that love and
respect were not commodities you could buy. And
without love and respect, at least in her book,
physical love was not possible.

She picked up the tray and carried it back into

the living room. He was leaning back smoking, his
long legs stretched out in front of him, his head
resting on the back of the couch.

Oh, he was attractive, she thought as she walked
towards him, watching him. The way the firelight
played about the hard planes of his face and lit up
the smooth black hair made him seem mysterious
and appealing. His eyes were half-closed and he
appeared to be relaxed and quite content.

Very sure of yourself, aren't you, Mr Curzon?
she thought as she set the tray down on the table.
But I'm immune to your seductive charm. She sat
down beside him, picked up a cup and handed it
to him, pleased to see how steady her hand was.

'Actually, what I wanted to talk to you about,'
she began calmly, 'was what I'm supposed to do
with myself. So long as you're determined to keep
me here, I'll need something to do.'

He straightened up and took the coffee cup
from her, giving her a quizzical look. 'Yes. I can
see that you wouldn't be satisfied with bridge clubs
and shopping expeditions. What did you have in
mind?'

'I don't know yet. I guess for now I just wanted
your permission.'

His cup clattered down on the table and he
turned abruptly towards her. 'My permission! My
God, woman, you're not a prisoner here.' As he
sat glaring at her, she could sense the anger boiling
in him just below the surface. His mouth was set in
a grim line, his eyes narrowed, and a muscle
worked in his jaw.

'That's nice to know,' she said quietly. 'I wasn't
sure just what my limits were.' She gave him an
innocent look over the rim of her cup as she took

a sip of coffee. 'I plan to go to church tomorrow with Mrs Varga, to begin with. There's always a need for volunteer workers there. You said I could have the use of a car.' She looked at him. He nodded briefly, his face still grim. 'Well, then,' she said with a smile, 'I'll start exploring the possibilities.'

The next morning, Cara and Mrs Varga set out early for church. Cara drove, wanting to get the feel of the late model sports car in the garage that Nicholas said she could use before venturing down the mountain into Reno.

Mrs Varga kept up a steady stream of chatter all along the way, gossip mostly about the parishioners and the inevitable conflicts. Cara concentrated on her driving and listened with only half an ear, making suitable comments from time to time so as not to offend the woman. She also had her mind on her conversation with Nicholas last night. It had definitely cleared the air for her. She knew now where matters stood, and this morning she had awakened for the first time since her marriage with a light heart and a sense of anticipation and hope for the future.

True to his word, Nicholas had left her strictly alone last night. After dinner, she had cleared the table and straightened up the kitchen, lingering over the familiar tasks as long as possible. When she had gone back into the living room, he had been banking up the fire, and when he'd finished, said he had work to do and would be in his study across the hall if she needed him for anything.

She had sat in front of the dying embers of the fire, then, reading the paper, alone with her thoughts. At ten, she had turned the lights out and gone to bed. As she had passed by the closed door of his study, she noticed a light burning underneath and hesitated, wondering if she should say good night to him.

No, she decided, passing on to her own room. It would be better to keep her distance in every way. It wasn't fair to him to make friendly overtures when she had no intention of carrying them through.

The chapel was a small one with room for about a hundred parishioners. Even then, it was only half-full. There was one Mass on Sunday morning, celebrated by one of the priests at St Margaret's in Carson City. Father Benedict was an elderly man with a thick Irish accent, a round innocent face and a wisp of white hair feathering over the top of his bald pink head.

After Mass, Cara lingered behind the others who stopped to chat with the priest in the vestibule where he was stationed, still in his alb and chasuble. She wanted to have a few words with him in private while Mrs Varga was busy chatting with her friends near the door. Finally, the last person left, and he was alone.

'Good morning, Father,' she said as she approached him. 'I'm Cara Curzon.'

He grasped her outstretched hand in both of his and beamed at her, his pale blue eyes twinkling. 'Ah, then, you'd be the new Mrs Nicholas, I take it.' She nodded, and he pumped her hand vigorously. 'Welcome, then, to Lake Tahoe, Mrs Curzon. Your husband has been very generous to our little parish. It's a great pleasure to meet you.'

'Thank you, Father,' she murmured, somewhat

taken aback to learn that Nicholas was a
benefactor of the church. 'May I speak to you for
a moment?'

'Of course, of course.'

'I'm new here to Lake Tahoe, as you know, and
find I have quite a lot of time on my hands. I'm
used to being busy, and I'd like to find something
useful to do. Is there anything you could suggest?'

He released her hand and cocked his head to
one side, then pursed his lips and gave her a long
appraising glance. 'Well, now,' he said, 'there's
certainly always a lot that needs doing. Will you
tell me what you had in mind? Perhaps the Ladies'
Guild?'

She shook her head frowning. 'No, Father,
nothing like that. I'm not looking for a social life.
I want to work.'

'Ah, then, let me tell you what we really need,
and you can think it over, perhaps let me know
next week how it strikes you.' They started
walking towards the front door. Everyone else had
gone, and Mrs Varga was waiting for her by the
steps. Father Benedict turned to Cara. 'You see,
what we really need most desperately you might
not be interested in.'

'Tell me what it is.'

'A few of the more stalwart women in the parish
have got together and set up a day care centre in
the chapel basement.' He gave her a sad smile.
'There's a lot of money around here, from the
gambling, you see, and although people are very
generous, like your husband, there's also a lot of
poverty. Not in a monetary sense, but in the sense
of quality time. Many of the young ladies who
perform in the shows at the big nightclubs have

small children, as do a lot of the women who work
the tables in the casinos. They work all night,
usually, and must sleep in the daytime. They're
well paid and can afford good care for their
children, babies, some of them, but who is going to
provide the care they need?'

Cara listened intently. Outside, the sky was
bleak and grey, and a cold damp breeze blew in
through the open doorway. She shivered a little in
her heavy woollen coat, thinking of the children
with no one to care for them except indifferent,
paid help.

'Well,' Father Benedict said after a time, 'what
do you think? Will you consider helping out with
our children and let me know next Sunday?'

'No,' Cara said firmly. 'I don't have to think
about it. I want to help. I'm not used to children,
but I think I could learn.'

He beamed at her. 'Well, now, that's what I call
a woman who knows her own mind. I'll tell you
what. You call our director and let her know
you're interested in helping out. She'll schedule a
time for you. I don't have her number offhand,
but she's in the Tahoe 'phone book. Diana
Hathaway, her name is, Mrs Robert Hathaway.
Perhaps you know her? They're great friends of
your husband.'

'Yes, of course,' Cara murmured. 'We've met.
Thank you, Father. I'll call her tomorrow.'

'Good, good. And God bless you, my dear.'

That afternoon the sun came out and Cara set out
on her usual walk down to the boat dock,
bundling up with woollen scarf, heavy jacket and
gloves against the chilly air. The water of the lake

drew her, a shadowy reminder of home and the ocean.

She leaned up against the railing and gazed down into the clear, still depths of the lake. It's very beautiful, she thought, but it still wasn't the ocean, with its raging power and vast expanse. She missed the smell of the sea, the salty tang of the breezes that blew from it. She missed the familiar screechings of the gulls, the great boulders that dotted the rugged coastline, the wide stretch of sandy beach.

Most of all, she missed her mother and the quiet serene life she had lived in their little cottage. All the opulence of her role as Mrs Nicholas Curzon could never make up for what she had lost. When she felt the hot tears stinging her eyes, she brushed them away angrily and stamped her foot on the wooden dock.

'No!' she muttered under her breath. 'I will not give in to self-pity. I did what I had to do, and I'll make the best of it.'

The pale sun went behind the clouds again. It would soon be dark, and rain was threatening again. As she walked slowly back to the house, she thought over her conversation with Father Benedict that morning. It would be good for her to have something to do, and she was looking forward to a useful occupation. It had surprised her to learn that Nicholas helped support the little chapel. Conscience money? she thought. A tax write-off? Surely a man like that would do nothing unless it was profitable in some way to him.

A light rain began to spatter on her face, and she quickened her step. As she neared the house, she could hear a strange noise coming from the back, an odd heavy sound, a regular staccato beat that broke the stillness.

When she reached the shelter of the overhanging eaves, she made her way slowly along the path at the side of the house to investigate, and as she did, the faint steady sound grew louder, until she came around to the back and saw Nicholas over by the garage.

He was chopping wood, his back to her. He had taken off his shirt, and his worn blue jeans hung low over his narrow hips as he methodically raised the axe over his head and then slammed it down to split the log at his feet, working in a steady rhythm.

Cara stared at him, rooted to the spot, mesmerised by the sight of the tall man, the taut firm muscles of his broad shoulders rippling as he expertly wielded the axe, the long bony ridge of his spine visible below the jeans as he bent over. Each time he finished a log, he piled the split pieces neatly in a stack against the garage, then lifted another heavy log and set it in place on the chopping block.

She couldn't take her eyes off him. The sheer beauty of his precise economical movements was like a graceful athletic dance. Each time he raised the axe high in the air, Cara caught her breath as the powerful sinews of his arms bunched and tensed, and the jeans slid a little lower around his hips.

She stood there watching him for several minutes. It was raining harder now, and his black hair was plastered wetly to his skull. When she saw him bury the axe in a nearby tree stump and reach for his heavy plaid woollen shirt that hung on a nearby tree limb, it dawned on her that he was getting ready to stop.

The sudden thought came to her that he mustn't know she'd been standing there watching him. Hurriedly she turned to go. But it was too late.

'Cara,' he called after her.

She turned around. He was walking slowly towards her, buttoning his shirt, and as he came closer she noticed the mingled sweat and raindrops glistening on his forehead and saw him raise an arm to wipe it with his sleeve. He was standing before her now, not a foot away, staring down at her, an inscrutable smile playing about his lips.

She was speechless, not only embarrassed that he had caught her watching him like that, but still disturbed by the sight of all that naked masculine flesh. He was so close to her that she caught the strong male scent of him, a combination of healthy perspiration, damp wool and freshly chopped wood.

She wondered how long he'd known she was there. Had he been putting on a show for her benefit? She searched her mind for a plausible explanation for her presence.

'I—I wanted to talk to you about something,' she finally managed to stammer.

He raised an eyebrow. 'Can it wait until I've showered and changed?' he asked easily.

'Of course,' she replied. She looked up at him. There was a faintly mocking, knowing look in those penetrating grey eyes. Then she thought, what difference did it make? Even if he suspected she'd been watching his 'show', he still couldn't be certain.

'I'll just cover the wood and put the axe away, then,' he said in an even tone.

She nodded coolly at him, turned, and continued

down the path to the kitchen entrance. All the while she had the uneasy feeling that he was staring at her retreating figure, but she checked the impulse to hurry, and made herself walk slowly and sedately, her head held high, until she was safely inside the house.

Mrs Varga had left for the evening, and when Cara had taken off her outdoor things, she went into the living room in her stockinged feet to build a fire. Chilled to the bone, she sat on the floor close to the warmth of the dancing flames while she waited for Nicholas.

She still had on the denim jeans and shabby white sweater she'd changed into after church, and, glancing down at them now, she thought about her scanty wardrobe. The clothes that had been adequate for her life in a fishing village would hardly be suitable for her new role as Mrs Nicholas Curzon, especially if she were to go ahead with her plan to help in the playschool at the chapel. She'd have to have some decent clothes, even if her stay was as short as she still hoped it would be. Having made up her mind, however, to make the best of the bad situation that she had, after all, entered into of her own free will, there was no point in embarrassing herself and Nicholas by looking like a cast-off waif.

She heard his footstep behind her, and looked up as he came into the room. He was freshly showered, his black hair still a little damp, and was wearing tan chino trousers and a dark brown sweater, with the open collar of his white shirt showing at the neck.

For a moment he stood quite still as his glance flicked over her. Then he sat down on the couch and reached out to pour himself a drink from the try on the coffee table.

'Would you like a drink?' he asked. 'A glass of wine?'

'No, thank you.'

Glass in hand, he leaned back on the couch and stretched his long legs out in front of him. He took a long swallow of his drink, his eyes still on her.

'What was it you wanted to talk to me about? It must have been important for you to track me down in the midst of my labours.'

His tone was mocking, and the implication clear. Cara fought down the impulse to snap at him and to assure him she wasn't at all interested in 'tracking him down'. If he was baiting her about watching him this afternoon, it would only add to his satisfaction if she denied it.

'As a matter of fact,' she said calmly, 'it is rather important, at least to me.'

He leaned his head back and closed his eyes. 'Well, let's have it, then.'

'I spoke to Father Benedict this morning after Mass,' she said carefully, 'and he told me the day-care centre needed volunteers to help with the children.' She paused and glanced over at him, but when he didn't speak, she went on. 'I told him I'd like to help out.' Still no response. 'I'd like your permission to call Diana Hathaway and offer my services. Apparently she's the head of it, and since the Hathaways are friends of yours, I thought I should ask . . .'

Before she could finish the sentence, Nicholas had sat bolt upright and was glaring down at her.

'I told you you weren't a prisoner here, Cara,' he bit out in a strained voice. 'You don't need my permission to conduct a normal life, for God's sake.'

She darted a quick look at him. He sounded as though he was only keeping his temper in check with an effort of will. And she also sensed the hurt beneath the anger. What did he expect? He says I'm not a prisoner, she thought, yet in fact, that's exactly what I am. She sighed. Nothing would be gained by labouring that issue. The man was a mystery to her. She had no idea how his mind worked. He seemed to be deliberately trying to keep it that way.

'All right,' she said at last. Then, 'I'll need some clothes.'

He nodded curtly. 'Of course. I already told you you could have anything you wanted.'

A wave of despair passed over her, and she struggled against it. Anything I want, she thought bitterly, except my freedom.

'Why don't you drive into town one day next week,' he went on. 'Meet me at my office and we'll go open a bank account for you. You won't have any trouble in Reno charging whatever you want, anyway.'

'All right,' she murmured. 'Thank you.' She stood up. 'Shall we have our dinner? Mrs Varga left a roast in the oven, and I think it must be about done.'

He drained his drink and rose to his feet. When she was almost at the door to the dining room, she heard him call to her. She turned around. He was standing with his back to the fire, his legs slightly apart, his head thrown back to reveal the long column of his neck over the open collar of his shirt.

'Cara,' he said softly. 'Get something pretty when you go shopping, will you?'

She opened her mouth to reply, longing to shout at him that the farthest thing from her mind was to look pretty for him, but she bit back the angry retort and simply nodded at him non-committally.

The next day, Cara called Diana Hathaway, who was delighted at the prospect of getting another volunteer.

'You have no idea how hard it is,' she said. 'Everyone wants to give money, but no one wants to give time. How often can you come?'

Cara had to laugh at the eagerness in her voice. 'As often as you need me. Mrs Varga runs the house like clockwork, and I don't dare interfere.'

'Marvellous,' Diana crooned happily. 'I'll work you to death with that kind of attitude.'

'You might not want me when you see me in action,' Cara warned. 'I've never been around small children or babies before.'

'Don't worry about that. I think you'll find you have a natural instinct for it. All women do, if they allow it to surface.' She chuckled. 'Besides, it'll be good practice for when you have your own.'

For a moment Cara couldn't speak. Her own children? Hardly, but she couldn't very well tell Diana that. 'Yes,' she said at last, 'there's that, too.'

They made arrangements to meet at the day-care centre on Wednesday afternoon. Cara needed a few days to do some shopping before she committed herself to a regular routine.

She spent the rest of the day going through her old clothes, most of which she folded neatly into a box that she put up on the shelf of her wardrobe. As she did so, she noticed the parcel Nicholas had given her on her wedding day, still well back on the shelf where she had put it that night. She'd forgotten all about it, and for a moment she was tempted to take out the beautiful white gown just to look at it again. She resisted the impulse firmly. It could stay up there until it rotted to shreds for all she cared.

Late that afternoon, she sat down at her dressing table with a notepad and pencil to draw up a list of the clothes she'd need. The task unnerved her. She'd given so little thought to what she wore all her life that she had no idea where to even begin.

Well, she thought at last, after staring at the blank page for a good half hour, I'll just concentrate for now on the basics I absolutely must have to get by. As for style, she'd stick to classics. At the Hathaways' party, the other women had worn every conceivable fashion. She'd buy only what she felt comfortable in. Nicholas had promised her before they married that he wouldn't interfere in her choice of clothes.

Finally, after another hour of concentration, she'd drawn up a list of essentials: a warm woollen suit with a few blouses and an extra skirt; at least one dress she could wear on social occasions besides her black wedding dress; a couple of pairs of shoes; maybe a winter dress coat to replace the shabby tan raincoat.

With a sigh of relief, she tore the page off the notepad and tucked it in her handbag so she wouldn't forget it tomorrow. She felt a little guilty about the money she'd have to spend, but

Nicholas was the one providing it, and he didn't seem to mind.

At the dinner table that night, she told Nicholas that she'd like to drive into Reno to do her shopping the next day and get it over with.

He gave her a curious look. 'You make it sound like some kind of penance, Cara. I thought women enjoyed shopping for clothes.'

She lowered her eyes to her plate. 'I haven't had much practice,' she said at last. Then, half-smiling, she looked at him. 'Don't encourage me,' she said drily. 'I might run amok and break you.'

He drew in his breath sharply and set his fork down carefully on his plate, his eyes fastened on her in an intense grey gaze. 'That's the first time I've seen you smile, Cara,' he said in a low voice. 'At least since we've been married.'

She winced at the reference, and immediately regretted her playful comment. I must never forget, she told herself, that this man is my enemy.

'I guess I haven't felt there was much to smile about,' she said quietly.

'I'm sorry about that,' he said softly. 'I remember how you used to smile. It was one of the things that attracted me to you in the first place, perhaps because it was so rare. You were always such a serious girl, and when you did smile, it was genuine, because something had really pleased you, and never out of politeness or the need to make an impression.'

Cara shifted uncomfortably in her chair. She didn't quite grasp the reason for his remarks, and they were far too personal to suit her. What could he mean? He almost made it sound as though he admired her, had admired her for a long time, for herself, who she really was deep inside, and not just as a body he wanted to possess.

If this were true, then why hadn't he simply been staightforward about it, even courted her, tried to win her love and respect rather than blackmail her into an unholy alliance against her will? It was on the tip of her tongue to ask him that question, but she remained silent. Of course, the answer was clear. He wasn't interested in her. He just wanted what he couldn't have.

When the silence lengthened, and it became clear that she wasn't going to reply, Nicholas picked up his fork and started eating again, and when he spoke, his voice was flat and dry.

'What time will you be coming into town?' he asked.

'Whenever it's convenient for you. I don't want to interrupt your work.'

'Considerate of you,' he said briefly. 'Such wifely concern is touching.' He pushed his chair back and threw his napkin down on the table. 'I'll expect you at the office, then, at eleven o'clock.' He gave her directions how to get there. 'We'll go to the bank, and if you think you can tolerate it, I'll take you to lunch.'

'All right,' she murmured.

She stared blankly down at her plate, unable to look at him. She hated conflict of any kind, and his sarcasm had cut deep. It occurred to her that her cold silence must have hurt him very much to evoke such a response.

In a moment, she heard him stalk out of the room. She raised her eyes and looked after his retreating figure. If only he would let me go, she thought in despair. We'll keep on hurting each other until he does.

CHAPTER SIX

THE next day Cara found the building where Nicholas had his office quite easily. Not only had he given her clear directions, but it was the tallest building in the small city and had the name, Curzon Building, lettered discreetly on a weathered bronze plaque near the entrance. She parked the car in the lot at the back and walked around to the front of the building.

She had almost decided not to come that morning. The weather had turned suddenly bitterly cold, and the sky was covered with a canopy of threatening-looking dull grey clouds. Nicholas had said they got snow in the winter at this altitude, but it was only just October. Surely it was too early. Since it rarely snowed on the Washington coast where she had lived all her life, she had no experience by which to measure the signs, and finally decided her hesitation was due more to her distaste for the shopping expedition than concern over the weather.

It seemed all right now, she thought as she made her way along the narrow pavement towards the entrance of the building. There was even a light sprinkling of rain, and that surely meant it was too warm to snow. Across the street in front of a bank was a reader board that flashed the time and temperature every few seconds. Thirty-five degrees, it said. Cold, but not freezing.

Somewhat reassured, Cara stepped in through the revolving door to the lobby. It was a very busy

106

place with lots of people bustling about, mostly men in business suits and efficient-looking women, a few delivery men in uniform. She felt strange and out-of-place. Everyone else looked so important with their briefcases and packages and stacks of paper, as though they were all on their way to crucial conferences. She also felt dowdy in her old tan raincoat, and was glad now she'd decided to get some better clothes.

The Curzon offices were on the tenth floor, and she found the bank of lifts right where Nicholas had told her they would be. She stepped inside an empty lift, punched the button, and the doors closed.

As she was borne slowly upward, she began to feel very nervous about appearing in Nicholas's office like this. She clutched her handbag tightly to keep her hands from trembling. She wished now she had arranged to meet him at the bank, but he had been insistent that she come here first.

One wall of the lift cage was covered with a sheet of opaque silvery glass, almost a mirror, and she glanced at her reflection apprehensively. Yes, she thought, making a face, definitely dowdy. The raincoat was shabby and ill-fitting. She tied the belt a little tighter. It helped a little. She took the white scarf off her head, smoothed back the thick mass of dark hair and tucked in a stray strand behind her ear. The heavy bun at the back of her head felt insecure, but it was too late to do anything about that now.

She wished she'd worn at least a touch of lispstick, but she didn't even own one. After a few experiments with make-up as a teenager, she'd given it up as too much trouble. Besides, in those days, she had been so confident that she would enter the convent that things like make-up and clothes had seemed superficial and unnecessary.

Well, it was too late now. The lift came to a stop, the doors slid open, and she stepped out into a large foyer. A thick beige carpet covered the floor, and the walls were hung with a neutral grasscloth. There were muted abstract paintings here and there in soft woodsy colours, with heavy draperies drawn at the sides of the windows that looked out on the surrounding mountains.

Directly in front of the lift, perhaps ten feet away, was a large neat desk, and sitting behind it was a very lovely, very crisp-looking blonde receptionist. She was dressed in a severely cut woollen dress of a dark blue material that looked as though it had cost the earth.

She was smiling as she spoke into a cream-coloured telephone, and jotting down notes with her free hand. As Cara approached her, she was uncomfortably aware of the appraising glance the blonde flicked her way, and she stood a little straighter, with her shoulders back, her chin up, willing herself to relax.

The receptionist hung up the telephone and looked up at Cara with a self-assured, slightly superior smile. 'May I help you?' she asked in a low pleasant voice.

'Yes, please,' Cara said. 'I'm Cara Curzon. I'm here to meet my husband.'

The sudden transformation in the blonde was so startling it was almost funny. The confident smile vanished. She sat bolt upright in her chair and immediately reached for the telephone again.

'Oh, yes, Mrs Curzon,' she said in a rush. 'Mr

Curzon is expecting you and told me to call him the minute you came in.' She punched a button on the telephone.

'I'm a little early,' Cara said hesitantly. 'I can sit down and wait if he's busy.'

'Oh, no,' the blonde said. Then she lowered her eyes and spoke into the receiver. 'Jerry, will you please tell Mr Curzon that his wife is here?'

She hung up the 'phone, openly staring at Cara now, who fought the impulse to fidget under that frankly curious gaze.

'He'll be right out,' she said at last.

'Thank you,' Cara murmured uneasily.

She wondered if she should just stand there or go sit down on one of the comfortable upholstered chairs against the wall. If Nicholas was busy, it could be a long wait. As she hesitated, a door opened behind the blonde receptionist, and Nicholas stepped into the foyer.

He looks so much taller, Cara thought, so much more solid somehow here in this impersonal atmosphere. He had on a charcoal grey three-piece suit, a crisp white shirt and a conservatively striped silk tie of grey and maroon. He looked very tanned, very handsome, and very impressive.

He walked towards her now in his long easy strides, one hand outstretched, a smile on his face. 'Cara,' he said. 'You're right on time.'

She smiled nervously at him. 'A little early, I'm afraid. If you're busy . . .'

'He took her hand in his. 'No, I'm just waiting for you.' He moved his hand to grasp her lightly by the elbow and turned to the blonde woman, who was openly goggling now, the cool sophisticated pose utterly abandoned. 'Cara, this is

Margaret Pierce, our very efficient—and very decorative—receptionist.'

Margaret actually blushed. She rose awkwardly to her feet, obviously flustered at the compliment from her boss. 'Yes, we've met. How do you do, Mrs Curzon?'

'I'm happy to meet you, Miss Pierce,' Cara said shyly.

'Come on, darling,' Nicholas said easily, grasping her elbow more firmly and guiding her to the door. 'I'll show you our offices and introduce you around, and then we'll have lunch.' He glanced back at Margaret, who was still standing there staring after them. 'Did you get those reservations all right?'

'Yes. The Russian Tea Room at twelve.'

He nodded, then led Cara down a long carpeted hall to a large open area at the very end of it. In the centre was another large wooden desk, this one covered with papers and files. A typewriter stand was attached to one side of it. Behind the desk sat a middle-aged rather plump woman with grey hair cut in a short mannish style and wearing a dark brown tailored suit and horn-rimmed glasses.

A stocky blond man was standing by the desk, a sheaf of papers in his hand. The two of them were deep in earnest conversation, but both looked up as Cara and Nicholas came towards them.

'Estelle, John, this is my wife.' Cara was surprised at the unmistakable note of pride and possessiveness in his voice. He put an arm around her waist and drew her towards the others. 'Cara, this is my secretary, Estelle Costanza, and my assistant, John Trenholm.'

More uncomfortably conscious than ever of her

shabby appearance, such a sharp contrast to all
the sartorial elegance and decorative splendour of
her surroundings, Cara shook hands and made
polite responses in a sort of numb, instinctive daze.

Nicholas led her then through another door,
closed it behind him, and immediately dropped his
arm from her waist. For a moment, Cara felt
bereft without his comforting touch in the midst of
such unfamiliar territory, but as she gazed around
the large imposing office, she soon forgot her
timidity.

'It's—very impressive,' she said at last.

The decor was similar to the rest of the floor
with the same colour carpet and walls. A large desk
looked out upon a view of the city and the
mountains beyond, and there were several comfortable chairs. No paintings were in here,
however, only two large framed photographs, one
of an old-fashioned building that had a sign saying
'Curzon's' on the front of it in large plain letters.
The other one, much to her amazement, was of a
section of the coastline near Southport, the
familiar row of fishing boats tied up at the dock in
the distance.

She could only stare at it in disbelief. It had never
occurred to her that the place would have such
significance to Nicholas that he would go to the
trouble of procuring and hanging such a picture in
his office.

She turned to face him. He was standing by the
window, leaning back against the wall, his arms
folded across his chest, and staring at her with a
look of peculiar intensity in his grey eyes, almost
as though it was very important to him to see her
reaction to the photograph.

'Surprised?' he said at last.

'Yes, a little. How long have you had it?'

'Let's see, must be five or six years now. It was taken from your father's boat.'

She didn't know what to say. There was an odd stillness in the quiet room, with only an occasional muffled sound coming from beyond the closed door, a telephone ringing, the distant clack of a typewriter, muted voices.

She looked back at the picture. It was all so familiar. A wave of homesickness passed over her, a longing to be back in that safe world again. What was she doing here in this strange town, this strange office, with this strange man? She felt oddly disorientated, as though she had awakened from a dream to find herself suddenly transported to another planet. She had the impulse to turn around and run. But where would she run to?

She closed her eyes, swaying a little, and reached out to a nearby chair to steady herself. There was a buzzing sound in her head, a blankness behind her eyes.

Then, dimly, she heard a muttered curse, hurried footsteps, and felt Nicholas's hand clutching her elbows, pulling her to him. She leaned up against his hard chest and felt his arms come around her, holding her tenderly, his large hands stroking her back in long soothing motions, his mouth on her forehead, against her hair.

'God, I'm sorry, Cara,' he muttered. 'I had no idea it would affect you that way.'

Gradually, she felt her strength return, and with it came a renewed surge of resentment towards this man who had forced her to leave everything that was familiar to her, everything she loved.

'Sorry! You're not sorry.' She stiffened and pulled away from him. 'Don't,' she said. 'Please don't touch me. Not now.'

His dark head snapped back as though she had struck him. His hand fell to his side, and he stepped away from her. Her eyes were just level with his chin, and she stared fixedly at the collar of his shirt, the knot in his striped tie, the tanned neck, the firm upthrust chin, and she could see a pulse working erratically along the line of his lower jaw.

'We'd better go,' he said at last in a stiff, lifeless tone. 'Our reservations are for twelve.'

'I'm not hungry.'

'Well, I am.' He grabbed her roughly by the elbow and started propelling her towards the door.

She opened her mouth to protest, but when she glanced up at him and saw the grim look on his face, her spirits sank. She was no match for his superior strength. His will was like iron, as powerful as the hand clutching her arm, and she had no doubt that he would carry her bodily to the restaurant and tie her to a chair if she resisted him now.

They marched down the long hallway, through the reception area and into the waiting lift. Not a word passed between them. In the lobby of the building, Nicholas maintained his firm grip on her and she almost had to run to keep up with his long strides.

It seemed much colder out in the street now than it had when she first arrived. There were even a few flakes of light powdery snow. For a moment, Cara forgot her anger and resentment at Nicholas. How in the world was she going to drive up that mountain?

They walked to the nearby restaurant, where Nicholas was greeted most effusively by name and led to a table near a window. Cara sat and stared blankly at the ornate, oversized menu, which listed no prices whatsoever. Sunk in misery, worried about the drive home, her stomach churning, there was nothing that appealed to her anyway. When the waiter appeared to take their order and asked if they wanted drinks, she only shook her head.

'I'll have a martini,' Nicholas said. 'A double.' He looked at her. 'Have you decided what you want for lunch?'

'I'm still not hungry.'

'I'll order for you, then.' His voice was steely and controlled.

When Cara heard him tell the waiter they would have steak sandwiches and salad, her stomach turned over again. She set the menu down and gazed out the window at the gently falling snow.

They sat in stony silence all through lunch. Cara picked at her salad and could eat only a few bites of sandwich. The way Nicholas polished off his double martini and consumed every bite on his plate with such relish killed what little appetite she had.

When he had finished, he leaned back, lit a cigarette and sighed with contentment. Cara pushed her plate away and glanced at him. He seemed quite relaxed after his hearty meal, she thought resentfully, and why not? He had everything he wanted.

He leaned forward and pulled the curtain of the window back with one finger. As he gazed out into the street, a frown appeared on his face, and he le the curtain fall. He beckoned to a passing waiter, who scurried over to their table instantly.

'Yes, Mr Curzon?'

'What are the road conditions up to the lake?'

'The most recent report is that chains are required.'

'What's the forecast?'

'It's supposed to freeze tonight, then warm up tomorrow.'

When the waiter left, Nicholas turned to Cara. 'You can't drive home this afternoon. You'll have to spend the night in town.'

She gave him a startled look. 'Where?'

'At the apartment.'

With him? She'd rather crawl up the road in the snow on her hands and knees. But before she could protest at the arrangement, he got to his feet and stood looking down at her, his mouth curled in a mocking smile.

'Don't look so tragic, Cara. There are two bedrooms.' He picked up the bill. 'Come on, now, let's get to the bank. You can do your shopping this afternoon, then come back to the office when you're through and I'll take you to the apartment.'

At the bank, Nicholas introduced her to Mr Curtis, the manager, who ushered them into his office with a great show of enthusiasm and courtesy. Cara just sat quietly in her chair and let Nicholas do all the talking. The two men seemed to be good friends, and she couldn't help noticing the contrast between her husband's easy manner with the banker and his stiffness whenever he spoke to her.

She signed her name wherever she was told to

and was presented with a cheque-book for
temporary use until her own personal cheques
were printed up. It was all over in fifteen minutes,
and when Nicholas rose to his feet, Cara stood up
and shook hands with Mr Curtis, then followed
Nicholas back out into the street.

Briefly, he pointed out some shops where she
could open charge accounts. 'Some of the better
ones are inside the big hotels,' he added. 'If you
have any trouble charging what you want, call me
and I'll take care of it.' Then, abruptly, he turned
and left her.

Doggedly and without much enthusiasm, Cara
took out the list she had made the day before and
headed towards the closest shop. She had very
little interest in the whole venture, but her
common sense told her she couldn't continue on
with her life in this place as Mrs Nicholas Curzon
without some additions to her wardrobe, and until
she could leave, she'd just have to play the game.
Her dowdy appearance only served to accomplish
the one thing she didn't want. It called attention to
herself, made her stand out. She cared nothing
about clothes for her own sake, but she did want
to fade as unobtrusively into the background as
possible. She realised that the only way she could
accomplish this was to dress the way everyone else
did and in a manner suitable for her station.

She opened the door of the shop and went
inside. She spotted a rack of suits against a wall
and began looking through them. They were very
lovely, but the prices were appalling. She gritted
her teeth and kept on. She'd just have to pay them,
that's all.

In a few minutes, a haughty blonde saleswoman

materialised and came towards her. 'May I help you?' she asked in a cold tone that clearly indicated her lack of interest in doing any such thing.

'Yes, please,' Cara said. She had found a dark red suit on the rack that she liked, a classic style that she could dress up or down, depending on the occasion. 'I'd like to try this suit on.'

The blonde gave her a sweeping glance, from head to toe, taking in the shabby raincoat, the worn shoes, the lack of make-up, the plain hairstyle. Her heavily-mascaraed eyes narrowed and she smiled superciliously.

'As you wish,' she said tightly. She reached for the price tag. 'This suit is priced at five hundred dollars.'

Cara felt a warm flush steal over the back of her neck. For an instant, she was tempted to turn around and run out the door. She glanced nervously at the saleswoman, whose make-up and hairstyle were so perfect she looked as though she would crack if you touched her. Condescension and contempt emanated from her in almost palpable waves. Cara began to grow angry.

'I'm aware of the price,' she said calmly. 'May I try it on?' She looked directly into the blonde's pale blue eyes, and was gratified to see a flicker of doubt there.

'Of course,' she said at last. She took the suit off the rack. 'This way, please.'

In the dressing room, Cara firmly declined her offer of assistance. When she tried the suit on, it fit perfectly. She called to the saleswoman and asked her to choose a selection of blouses and an extra skirt. After another half hour, she ended by choosing two blouses, a lovely silk scarf, a sweater, and a finely woven black and red tweed skirt that would go well with the suit jacket.

When the blonde carried her selections off, Cara got dressed in her old clothes and went back out to the counter. She knew that by now her purchases added up to a sizable sum of money. As she watched the saleswoman wrap her parcels and write out the sales slip, Cara was still uncomfortably aware of the woman's obvious distaste. She was very silent, her painted lips set in a firm line, and she kept darting suspicious looks at her. Since Cara had to either charge her purchases or pay by cheque, she knew there would be an unpleasant confrontation, and she steeled herself for it.

'And how would you like to pay?' the blonde asked in saccharine tones when she had finished and announced the staggering total.

'I'll charge it,' Cara said firmly.

The blonde's eyes widened. 'What name?'

'Mrs Nicholas Curzon.'

The pale eyes almost popped out of their sockets, then narrowed in suspicion. 'Do you have some identification?'

'No, I'm afraid not.' Everything she owned was in her maiden name.

'Then I'll have to verify it.'

Cara nodded. 'Please do.'

She disappeared into the back of the store. When she returned after a few minutes, the haughty look had vanished. She appeared shattered, virtually a broken woman. Cara smiled to herself. She could well imagine just how Nicholas would 'deal' with her.

'Will you please just sign here, Mrs Curzon?' she requested in humble tones. 'Thank you very much. I must apologise for the delay. Please come in again. If there's anything I can do for you, anything at all . . .'

She went on and on in that vein, to the point where Cara almost believed she preferred the haughtiness. Finally, she made her way out the door, clutching her parcels, the blonde following her every inch of the way.

She spent the rest of the afternoon shopping for shoes, underwear, a heavy coat, even a little make-up, becoming acquainted with the stores and methodically going down her list. After that initial experience, she felt more confident in dealing with salespeople, and by five o'clock she had an armload of packages, as well as a sizable bill for her husband to pay.

She trudged wearily back to the office at last to find Nicholas waiting for her in the lobby of the building by the lifts. When he saw her stagger inside juggling packages, he stepped quickly towards her, took the heavier packages out of her aching arms, and gave her a cool smile.

'I see you took me at my word,' he said. 'You look exhausted.'

'I am,' she said with feeling as she handed him yet another parcel. 'Shopping is even harder work than I thought. I can see now why I've always avoided it.'

He led her out the back entrance to the parking lot, where his silver Mercedes was parked. He unlocked the door and piled her packages in the back seat, then opened the passenger door for her.

'We'll leave your car here overnight,' he said

when he got in beside her. 'It'll be safe, and there's plenty of antifreeze in the radiator.'

As he started the car and they drove off, Cara leaned her head back and closed her eyes. Her feet were sore, her back ached, her arms were stiff, and she was exhausted. She also recognised the faint stirrings of hunger, and by the time Nicholas pulled into the underground garage of a large apartment building, she realised she was ravenous.

They hadn't spoken on the short drive. When he shut off the engine, Cara opened her eyes to find him gazing intently at her. She sat up straight and smoothed her skirt. Quickly he looked away.

'You look beat,' he said as he opened his door. 'Let's go up now. A hot bath will do wonders for you. I'll come back down for your things while you're soaking.'

She nodded and got out of the car, then followed him to the lift. His apartment was on the top floor. In fact, she realized, when they stepped out into a wide foyer, it *was* the top floor.

She was too tired then to really take in her surroundings, but as she followed Nicholas down a long hallway, she was vaguely aware of a feeling of opulence and quiet luxury in the furnishings and decor. They came to a bedroom, and she breathed a sigh of relief when she saw a large comfortable-looking bed.

Nicholas showed her the adjoining bathroom. 'Everything you need should be here somewhere,' he said as he moved back towards the door that led into the hall. 'I won't disturb you. Lie down for a while if you feel like it.'

'Thank you,' she said. 'It looks wonderful.' She

smiled at him, then, but he was gone, the door closed quietly behind him.

She turned and eyed the bed longingly. No, she said firmly to herself. A bath first. She went into the bathroom, turned on the tap in the gleaming bath, and wearily began to undress.

When she awoke, it was pitch dark in the bedroom. She experienced a momentary sensation of disorientation and sat bolt upright in the bed. Then it came to her where she was, and she let her head fall back down again on the pillows.

What time was it? She rolled over and switched on the bedside lamp, blinked in the sudden glare, and glanced at her watch. It was eight o'clock. She'd slept for two hours. Her stomach ached and growled with hunger. She sat up again, her eyes more accustomed to the light now, and glanced around.

Piled neatly in a corner of the room were the largest of her packages. Other smaller ones were stacked on a nearby table. She glanced down at the warm eiderdown that covered her. After her bath, she had put her slip back on and laid herself down on top of the bed. Nicholas must have covered her when he came in with the packages.

She jumped off the bed and padded barefoot to the wardrobe, where she had hung her dress earlier. It looked very shabby and forlorn in the vast empty space.

She had unpinned her hair, and it hung loosely now about her shoulders. After she put on her dress, she went to the mirror over the dresser and twisted it back up again in her neat chignon. She glanced at the packages, wondering whether she should unpack them, but decided there was no point. Hopefully, tomorrow she'd be able to drive home.

She opened the bedroom door and stood there listening for a moment. It was very quiet. She walked down the hall to the living room. A dim lamp was burning by a large sofa, but Nicholas was nowhere in sight. It was too early for him to have gone to bed. Had he gone out?

She continued to explore until she came to a small kitchen. She smelled food, and her stomach growled hungrily. There was a note taped to the oven door, in Nicholas's slashing black script: 'Casserole warming in oven. Salad in refrigerator. If you need me for anything, I will be working in my study.' It was signed with the single letter 'N'.

She dished up a plate of food and sat at the small table to eat. It was very good, and she wondered if Nicholas had prepared it or if Mrs Varga kept the freezer stocked for him. There was a pot of coffee on the stove, and when she had finally satisfied her ravening hunger, she poured herself a cup. She set it on the table to cool while she rinsed her dishes off in the sink and stacked them in the dishwasher under the counter. Inside were another plate, a few glasses, a cup and saucer. Nicholas must have eaten earlier.

As she sat back down at the table to drink her coffee, she heard muffled footsteps behind her. She turned around to see Nicholas standing in the doorway. He was wearing the dark trousers to his suit, and his white shirt was open at the collar, the sleeves rolled up over his wrists. He looked a little drawn and tired. The network of lines around his eyes were more deeply etched, and the high cheekbones seemed more prominent. His hair was ruffled, with one dark strand falling over his forehead.

He came closer into the light. 'Are you finding everything you need?' he asked.

'Yes, thank you. I'm fine.'

He glanced at her cup. 'Do you mind if I join you?'

'No. Of course not.' She half-rose out of her chair, an automatic response from her years of waiting on her father and brothers.

'Sit down,' he said. 'I'll get it.'

As he spoke, she became aware for the first time of his wide, finely carved mouth. The lips were thin, but well-shaped, and very sensitive. Once again, too, she noticed how economical and graceful his movements were as he reached up into the cupboard, walked over to the stove, lifted the pot.

He sat across from her then and lit a cigarette. 'I'm sorry you had a problem with that saleswoman today,' he said. 'By the time I got through with her, she should have been a model of courtesy to you.'

Cara couldn't help smiling. 'I can't really blame her. She was bound to be suspicious of anyone who looks like I do walking in and claiming to be Mrs Nicholas Curzon.' He didn't say anything. 'I thought of paying by cheque, but we'd have had to go all through the same thing anyway.'

He only nodded. 'Did you find everything you needed?' he asked at last.

'Isn't it obvious?' she said lightly. 'I felt like a criminal spending all that money. It would keep my whole family for a long time.'

His face hardened. 'Your family is taken care of, and I told you to spend whatever was necessary.'

He drained the last of his coffee, stubbed out his cigarette and pushed his chair back. He got up and took his cup over to the sink, rinsing it out and putting it in the dishwasher, all very neatly and methodically.

At the door, he turned around. 'I'll say good night now. You should be able to amuse yourself. There are books and magazines in your bedroom, and television if you're interested. The weather forecast looks promising. It's supposed to warm up by morning. You won't have any trouble driving up to the lake. You can ride into the office with me in the morning and pick up your car.'

He was gone before she could even say good night.

When Cara woke up the next morning, the sun was shining palely through the heavy curtains at the window. It was eight o'clock. She'd read for a while last night in bed, then turned the light off around midnight and gone right to sleep again.

She jumped out of bed and dressed again in her old clothes. As she washed and brushed her teeth, she caught herself thinking with some anticipation and even a little longing of the new clothes she had bought yesterday. She smiled at her reflection in the bathroom mirror. Was she becoming corrupted by the fleshpots of Reno? Would she change into one of those women whose appearance was their whole life?

No, she decided. She'd never do that. She reminded herself that she was only playing a part, acting in a play, biding her time until the day came when Nicholas would let her go. He had seemed quite cool towards her yesterday, distant and polite. Perhaps that meant he was getting tired of the charade he had forced her into, even ready to give it up, and she felt a little surge of hope.

When she went out into the hall, she could smell freshly brewed coffee and hear sounds coming from the direction of the kitchen. As she walked towards it, she passed by an open door and glanced inside. It was a rather spartan bedroom. There was a neatly made bed, and she could smell a faint steamy residue of masculine soap coming from the adjoining bathroom. Nicholas's room, she thought, and quickened her step.

In the kitchen, Nicholas was sitting at the table reading a newspaper and eating his breakfast. He was dressed in a different suit this morning, dark blue, beautifully cut and tailored to his long, lean frame. He had on a clean white shirt, another discreetly striped tie, and was freshly shaven.

He looked up from the paper when he heard her come in. 'Good morning,' he said gravely. 'Would you like some breakfast?'

'I'll just make some toast,' she said, stepping inside.

He nodded and went back to his paper. By the time Cara had drunk a glass of juice, buttered her toast and poured herself a cup of coffee, he had moved to the sink and was rinsing out his dishes.

'I'll take your packages down to the car,' he announced on his way out.

She gave him a nervous glance. 'Thank you. I'll only be a few minutes.'

It was on the tip of her tongue to ask him why he had brought them up in the first place. He could just as well have left them in the car. Then it occurred to her that perhaps he had hoped she would model her new clothes for him. By then he was gone anyway, and she finished her breakfast alone.

He hardly spoke to her at all on the way back to the parking lot of his office building. He had the radio tuned in to the weather report, and although the temperature was still below freezing in the higher elevations, Nicholas told her that the roads would be well-sanded by now.

'Just drive carefully,' he said after he had stowed her parcels in the back seat of her car.

He was standing outside and bending down to speak to her through the open window. There was a little wind, and it blew his neatly combed black hair about. He smoothed it back casually, straightened up and waited for her to start the car.

As she drove away from him and turned into the main road, she glanced into the rearview mirror. He was reflected there, standing quite still, his hands in his trousers pockets, his hair blown about by the wind, and even at this distance she could clearly make out the dark brooding look on his face.

CHAPTER SEVEN

CARA sat at the elegant secretary desk in the living room of the house at the lake gazing out the window at the gently falling snow. It was late November, almost Christmas, and she was addressing cards from the list Nicholas had given her. She glanced down at the stack of elegant red-and-gold cards. The sentiment expressed inside had surprised her when he'd handed them to her that morning. 'For God so loved the world He gave his only begotten Son.' Beneath the verse was printed 'Cara and Nicholas Curzon'.

She had been at Lake Tahoe for almost three months now, since the middle of September, and although her earlier hatred and resentment of the man she'd married had abated somewhat, she still didn't feel like his wife or think it was possible she ever would. The sight of her name linked with his on the card only made her feel sad and lonely.

Still, she thought, as she bent to her task once again, her marriage to Nicholas Curzon hadn't turned out to be quite the purgatory she had anticipated. She still missed her family, but she spoke to her mother at least once a week on the telephone and was planning a trip home after the holidays, with Nicholas's consent.

Home. Somehow the little village of Southport no longer seemed like home to her. Where do I belong? she wondered. By now she had become deeply involved at the church day-care centre,

127

spending almost every afternoon there. She loved the children, and she and Diana Hathaway had become good friends.

It was late afternoon and growing dark. From the kitchen she could hear Mrs Varga's radio playing softly and the sounds of cooking as she prepared their evening meal. A fire burned in the grate, and the room was cosy and warm.

Nicholas would be home soon. The snowplough had cleared the road to the lake that afternoon. He was a careful driver, familiar with the road and had snow tyres on the car. There was no danger. Occasionally he would stay in town in the apartment if he worked very late and would have to drive home in the dark, but he always let her know.

In spite of the settled pattern of her life, it still didn't seem real to her that he was her husband. And, in a way, she thought, he really wasn't. True to his word, he hadn't approached her since that last night when once again she'd turned from him retching with nausea. Her cheeks still burned at the memory. How his pride must have been damaged!

Somehow, though, she could no longer work up as much satisfaction at the thought of his bruised male vanity as she used to. He had been kindness itself to her in every way, never warm, granted, but never critical or accusing, either. What she couldn't understand was why he hadn't given up on her long ago and sent her home. He was a gambler, she thought. Surely he knew when to cut his losses.

Then she heard the sound of his car crunching on the snow-packed driveway, his feet stamping on the front porch and his key turning in the lock. When he opened the front door, a gust of cold air came in with him. She sat and waited, knowing he would come in the living room to have a drink before he showered and changed for dinner.

He came inside after he'd hung his coat up, rubbing his cold hands and went directly to the fire. 'How are you?' he asked, warming his hands over the flames.

'I'm fine.' She looked at him. 'Did you have any trouble on the road? It's been snowing steadily for some time.'

'No. No problem.' He came over to the desk and stood looking down at the stack of envelopes she'd been addressing.

'I thought you might decide to stay in town.'

She often wondered if he was alone on those nights, but had never dared to ask. It was none of her business, after all. He was a virile, attractive man and undoubtedly used to feminine companionship. Just because she didn't want him didn't mean other women wouldn't. She thought of the glamorous Moira Faraday and her blatant invitation to him the first night she'd met her at the Hathaways' party.

He only raised an eyebrow. 'I told you I'd be home. I would have called to let you know if I'd decided to stay in town.' He picked up a card. 'How are you coming with these? I could have had one of the girls in the office do them.'

'Oh, no,' she replied quickly. 'I don't mind. I like to have something to do.'

'It seems to me you have plenty to do with your day-care children.' He walked away from her towards the drink cabinet. 'Would you like a drink?'

She was about to give him her usual negative

reply. Every night he asked, and every night she refused. Tonight, however, for some reason, she felt like having a drink with him.

She stood up. 'Yes, please. I think I will. A glass of sherry.'

When he brought the drinks, they sat on the couch in front of the fire. She sipped her wine and watched him out of the corner of her eye. He was leaning forward, his long legs apart and his elbows resting on his knees. He looked tired, she thought. His face seemed drawn and his dark eyes were brooding as he gazed into the flickering flames. He seemed to be deep in thought.

Finally he turned to her. 'How would you feel about having a party?'

She stared at him. 'Here?'

'Yes. We've been to a few and I owe quite a lot of other people, and should do something for them over the holidays. If it sounds like too much trouble we can go to the casino, but Mrs Varga would help, and I'd like very much to do it here.'

She thought it over. Her first reaction had been to object. She knew nothing about giving parties. Then she looked around the large, beautifully furnished living room, the adjoining dining room, and the more she considered the idea, the more attractive to her it seemed. It might even be fun.

She turned to him with a smile. 'Yes,' she said. 'I'd like that. I don't have much experience as a hostess, though. I only hope I won't disgrace you.'

As she smiled at him, she saw the expression on his face gradually change from a distant aloofness to a tentative answering smile. It was as though a mask had slipped. For a second, the dark eyes burned with something like hunger, and he lifted a hand towards her, as if to touch her face. She held her breath. Then he drew it back quickly, and the polite mask settled on his face again. He turned away from her.

'I'll make up a guest list, then,' he said coldly. 'You can choose a date that suits you, but I'd like it to be before Christmas and preferably on a Saturday night.'

Christmas was only four weeks away, and Cara chose the second Saturday night before it for the party. The very next day after her talk with Nicholas, she bought the invitations and mailed them. She knew that if she didn't do it right away she'd get cold feet and try to back out of it. She was afraid it was rather late to ask people to a party during such a busy season, but within the next week almost every one of the forty people she had invited called to accept. Many of them were couples, but Nicholas had several single friends as well.

She knew the high acceptance rate was due mainly to the fact that an invitation to the Curzon house was a coveted prize in the social circles they travelled in, but she was also well aware that many of these people were simply curious about her. She was something of an anomaly at the lake. Married to one of the richest and most prominent men, she still stayed out of the limelight and maintained a low profile. Although her taste had vastly improved over the shabby clothes she'd arrived in, she dressed very conservatively, wore no jewellery and very little make-up. While most of the other wives were involved in bridge clubs and shopping expeditions, she lived very quietly and steered clear of the several purely social circles she could have joined.

The day of the party, Cara started out with a crisis of nerves, certain she could never go through with such an enormous undertaking. She had so much to do, however, to get ready for the party, that by early evening she was amazingly calm and very tired. The house looked lovely. She and Nicholas had gone out early to cut pine and fir and holly branches. Later, she had decorated the mantelpieces and tables in the living room and den with them, and it smelled fresh and woodsy indoors. She'd ordered several red, white and pink poinsettia plants and had placed them on the hearths and on the floor of the tiled entry hall. There was to be a buffet supper at midnight, and a large bouquet of red carnations was set in the middle of the dining-room table. Mrs Varga had been cooking and baking all day, and Cara had left the choice of what to serve entirely up to her.

Across the wide entry hall from the living room was a large, seldom-used den with a billiard table at one end and a fireplace at the other. Cara had decorated this room, too, and set up several tables and chairs around, nightclub-fashion for drinking and snacking. There was ample space in the den for dancing, and Nicholas had moved a small stereo set in for the music.

The guests were due to arrive at eight o'clock. At seven, Cara took one last look around to make sure she hadn't forgotten anything. Satisfied at last, she went to her room to get ready. She'd bought a new dress, cut in the usual conservative style, and as she surveyed herself in the bedroom mirror, she wondered a little dejectedly if she shouldn't have chosen something a little more festive. The material was a heavy pale blue velveteen, and she had chosen a size larger than she usually wore because the style was so form-fitting. The tight sleeves came down to her elbows, and even though the square neckline was a little lower than she normally wore, the total effect was demure rather than provocative.

Even with a new dress, she thought, I'll still look like a frump compared to the other women, who she knew would be dressed in their most glamorous holiday finery. Women like Moira Faraday, she mused. Then she thought of Diana Hathaway, plump and middle-aged, and she felt a little better. She wasn't trying to compete with Moira Faraday, anyway. If that's what Nicholas wanted, he was welcome to her. After all, she didn't want him. Moira could have him.

It dawned on her then that she was reacting just like a jealous wife, and she stared at her reflection in the mirror, wide-eyed, aghast. Why was she even thinking such thoughts? What had Nicholas ever said or done to lead her to believe he was even remotely interested in Moira? And why did she care? She shook her head and reminded herself once again that she was only biding her time until she could leave and go back home.

She swept out of the room. The guests would be arriving soon. She would play hostess for Nicholas, but she would keep in mind that it was only a part, a game. Probably she'd made a mistake to agree to the party in the first place, but it was too late now.

Nicholas had set up a bar in the den, and she found him in there now emptying ice into a silver bucket and checking the rows of glasses and bottles on the top of the counter. He looked up when she came into the room, and for a moment she was certain she saw a flicker of disappointment in his eyes as he silently took in her appearance.

She lifted her chin and continued walking towards him, reminding herself once again that she had no interest in his opinion. She dressed to please herself, not him. That had been part of their original bargain. He himself, she thought, looked dazzling in a white dinner jacket, black trousers and black dress tie, just like an ad in a glosssy magazine for the man of distinction. Heavy gold cufflinks flashed at the cuffs of his crisp white shirt, brilliant against the dark hair and skin of his face.

'You look very nice,' he said politely as she approached him.

Not beautiful, she thought, not lovely, just nice. 'Thank you,' she said, and was about to return the compliment, but caught herself just in time, warning herself to keep a distance between them.

'Are you nervous?' he asked.

'No,' she replied. 'Not at all.'

'That's good,' he said a little grimly. 'Although I can't imagine why you should be. These people mean nothing to you, after all.'

He was clearly including himself in that category, and she was a little stung. He made her sound so heartless and unfeeling. He was the one who had dragged her here against her will. She opened her mouth to remind him of this when the doorbell rang, and the first guests began to arrive.

From then on, she was too busy to give a

thought to Nicholas's opinions or her attitude towards him and his friends. She was kept busy all evening, helping Mrs Varga in the kitchen, making sure everyone had what they needed and spending some time with each guest as he or she arrived.

After the first few rounds of drinks, everyone began to loosen up. They all knew each other quite well and were comfortable together, so that there were no awkward blank spots in conversation. In fact, the den had grown quite noisy. The stereo was on, and a few couples were dancing. With all the preliminaries taken care of and the supper all ready to set out later, Cara finally was able to make her way to one of the small tables in the den where the Hathaways had just sat down after a particularly energetic spell of dancing. She was feeling a little tired, and her feet hurt in her new high-heeled shoes.

'Can I get you anything?' she asked, smiling at the red-faced Robert.

He mopped his bald head with his handkerchief. 'Not unless you have a magic elixir that will take ten years off me.'

'And about twenty pounds,' commented his wife drily.

He made a face at her. 'Look who's talking,' he jeered.

They smiled fondly at each other, and Cara felt a little stab of envy at their easy, relaxed manner with each other. She sat down at a vacant chair. Since she felt more comfortable with the Hathaways than any of the others, she had saved her hostess' visit with them for last so as not to slight anyone else by showing them preference.

Robert turned to her with a warm smile. 'Diana

tells me you're practically running the day-care centre singlehanded these days, Cara.'

She laughed. 'Hardly. I do enjoy it very much, though. I think it's so sad that those children live such unsettled lives. Most of them don't have fathers, or have had such a succession of stepfathers and "uncles" that they have no idea what family life is all about.'

'Sounds as though you believe pretty strongly in the value of family life, then,' he remarked. 'Is your own family a close one?'

'Oh, yes. I have three older brothers, and although they have to work hard with my father on the boats and never had much time for me, I always felt close to them.'

'Well,' Diana put in kindly, 'I'm sure you miss them, especially your mother. But one of these days you and Nick will have your own family, God willing, and that will keep you busy.'

The music started up again just then, loud and fast, saving her from having to comment on that unlikely prospect, and she turned to watch the dancers. Everyone seemed to be having a good time, and she was satisfied the party was a success.

She glanced at her watch. It was almost eleven. Mrs Varga had volunteered to stay until she'd served the buffet supper at midnight. Cara got up from the chair.

'I'd better go and see if Mrs Varga needs some help,' she said.

She turned to go, and almost collided with Nicholas, who was approaching the table. He held out his hands to steady her. She noticed that Moira was close behind him, dressed in a clinging scarlet dress held up by tiny straps. A deep vee neckline revealed a good portion of her full, round breasts.

'Where are you off to?' Nicholas asked. He released her arms. 'We were just coming over to join you.'

'I thought I'd go check on the supper,' she said.

'Nonsense. Sit down. Mrs Varga is perfectly capable of handling it herself. She'd probably only resent your interference.' He pulled out a chair. 'Come on. Sit down. Enjoy your own party.'

She sat. To have refused would have caused a scene. Nicholas pulled out a chair for Moira and another one for himself. Cara was feeling quite weary by now anyway, and Nicholas was probably right about Mrs Varga. It felt good to sit back and relax. The others chatted for a while about mutual friends and local gossip, and Cara just listened, smiling pleasantly, but not really entering into the conversation.

She was sitting between Robert and Diana across the table from Nicholas and Moira, who had moved her chair so close to his that another inch and she'd be in his lap. She was leaning towards him, listening raptly to his every word as he spoke, and Cara couldn't help noticing the bemused glances he kept darting into the interesting cleavage displayed so blatantly and obviously for his benefit. The gleam in his dark eyes told Cara that he was by no means immune to the beautiful blonde's seductive charms.

She had noticed, too, during the earlier part of the evening, that Moira wasn't the only woman at the party who seemed to find Nicholas attractive. To be fair, she had to admit that although he was courteous and friendly to all his guests, he never seemed to invite their intimacies himself, or appear overly attentive to any of them.

Women seemed to like to touch him. Whenever she had watched them talking to him during the evening, they always seemed to have a hand on his arm or fingers at his lapel or straightening his tie.

Once again, Cara reminded herself that she didn't care. So he had his pick of willing women. Well, all that meant to her was that he'd leave her alone. It was nothing to brood about. It wasn't her affair.

She looked over at him again. Moira was speaking now, and he had his head bent slightly towards her, listening to the low throaty tones that seemed to be meant for him alone and to consist of an amusing anecdote out of their mutual shared past. His eyelids were lowered, and a half-smile played about his lips. When Moira gestured in the air, making her point, he threw his head back and laughed.

Cara began to grow angry, especially when she saw his eyes return to fasten once again on the deep valley revealed by Moira's low-cut dress. She *didn't* care, she told herself again, but did he have to be so obvious about his interest in her?

He had been the one who'd wanted the party, after all, and the least he could do was to show her the consideration due her in public as his wife.

She felt she couldn't sit there another minute and watch him ogling Moira's cleavage. She started to rise, plastering a fake smile on her lips. Just then, then the music began again, a slow tune, and Nicholas got up and held a hand out to her.

'Dance with me, Cara,' he said.

She started to move away. 'No,' she said quickly. 'I have to see to the food.'

'Oh, for God's sake, Cara,' came Moira's nasal drawl. 'Will you please dance with him? You know damn well he won't dance with anyone else until you do.'

Cara was shocked. She stared at Moira, who gave her a disgusted look. Then she glanced at Nicholas. His mouth was set in a firm line. He seemed angry, but she couldn't tell if it was directed at her or at Moira. Was Moira right? she wondered. She hadn't even noticed, but now that she thought about it, she realised she had never seen him dance with anyone. He always asked her. She always refused.

'I'm sorry,' she stammered. 'I didn't realise.' She looked helplessly at Nicholas. 'Please dance with Moira, Nicholas. I don't mind, honestly.'

'I want to dance with you,' he said in a dead even tone, holding her gaze with his.

She looked up at him with troubled eyes. 'Nicholas,' she said in a low pleading voice. 'Please. I don't know how to dance.'

Relief washed over his face, and he smiled crookedly. He took her by the hand. 'Well, if that's all it is, it's easily remedied. Come on. I'll teach you.' He led her out on to the dance floor and gathered her into his arms. 'Just relax and follow me. Go with the music.'

It turned out to be far easier than she'd expected, and in just a short time she found she was quite enjoying herself. He held her firmly with his right arm around her waist, her hand clasped in his, guiding her around the dance floor with sure, expert steps. It felt good to lean against his strong length. She laid her head on his shoulder and closed her eyes, drifting light as a feather in his arms, his thighs pressing against hers.

When they first began to dance, he had placed her left hand on his shoulder, but little by little it had crept up around his neck. When she touched his skin, she felt his arm tighten around her, pulling her closer to him. She didn't resist. She had entered a dreamy, trancelike state, so tired from all her hostess duties that she was blissfully content just to float in his strong arms.

She forgot that this man was her enemy, that he had taken her virtually by force from her home, that her one goal in life was to get away from him. All she knew was what she felt at this moment. Safe, secure, cared for by the tall man who held her.

The music stopped, but still he held her. Cara opened her eyes and looked up at him. There was a half-smile playing about his finely chiselled lips, and his dark eyes were hooded as they fastened on hers. Even though she was aware of the others around them, it was as though they were all alone in the room. She had no desire to break away from him and his protective warmth.

Suddenly, a loud voice and the sound of laughter broke into her bewitched state. She stiffened and turned slightly in his arms to see what was going on.

Robert Hathaway stood behind her, pointing up to the ceiling and laughing a little drunkenly. He had been dancing with Moira, and she appeared to be sharing the joke with him.

'A kissing ring!' Robert shouted. He made a sweeping gesture with his arm towards Nicholas and Cara. 'Come on, newlyweds. Do your stuff.'

Cara raised her eyes. A branch of mistletoe, fashioned into a ring and tied with a red ribbon, had been suspended from the ceiling of the den. She and Nicholas were standing directly under it. She hardly had a moment to wonder who could have tacked it up there, when she felt Robert Hathaway's hand on her back, pushing her closer towards Nicholas.

She glanced around. A small circle of people had formed around them, smiling, laughing, their drinks held high, cheering them on. She gazed up at Nicholas, as though seeking direction.

'Chin up, darling,' he murmured with a reassuring smile. 'It looks as though we'll have to perform.'

She watched, wide-eyed, as his head bent down towards her, then felt his arms enfolding her tightly, drawing her up against him, and his cool lips on hers. Startled, she wasn't quite sure what to do, but the fleeting thought passed through her mind that the one thing she couldn't do was cause a scene. In spite of their past hostilities, Nicholas represented the one place right now where she felt safe from the several pairs of eyes that were openly goggling at them.

She slid her arms around his neck. His lips moved against hers, and she was surprised at how good it felt, how right it seemed. Then he raised his head, slid his hands up to her shoulders and squeezed them.

'Merry Christmas, Mrs Curzon,' he said with a smile. 'That was very nice.'

There was instant applause among their admiring audience and several murmurs of appreciation. The music started up again. Cara was still a little stunned by the whole affair, the discomfiture she felt at being the centre of attention, her pleasurable reaction to his kiss, and when Nicholas reached out for her again, it seemed like the most natural thing in the world to let herself sink towards him.

Just then, however, out of the corner of her eye, she saw Moira moving towards them. Without a glance at Cara, she put a hand on Nicholas's arm and stepped between them. Then she turned and gave Cara a saccharine smile, like a cat who has just swallowed the cream.

'Now,' Moira said with deep satisfaction. 'Now it's my turn.'

Cara jumped back as though she had been burned. She understood quite well that Moira had only been waiting for the opportunity to dance with Nicholas herself, and that she had virtually pushed Cara out on to the dance floor with him to achieve just that purpose.

'Of course,' Cara murmured, forcing out a polite smile. She couldn't look at Nicholas. 'I really must see to the supper anyway.'

Then she heard Nicholas's voice. 'Don't I have anything to say about this arrangement? I was dancing with my wife.'

She forced herself to meet his eyes. They were cold and distant. What was wrong with him? What did he expect her to do, fight over him with this woman who was so determined to dance with him? The dark gaze was challenging, asking a silent question. She hesitated. They were both watching her now. She didn't know what to do, but she had no intention of forcing the issue with Moira.

She smiled uncertainly and backed off a step. Then

she saw Nicholas drop his gaze and smile down at
Moira, whose arms had already slipped up around
his neck.

'All right, then, Moira,' he said, pulling her
closer. 'If my wife won't dance with me, I guess I'll
have to settle for you.'

'Beast!' Moira cried, her eyes sparkling with
laughter. 'You know you love it.'

They exchanged an intimate smile, born of long
and close friendship, and danced off, leaving Cara
standing there alone. Nicholas never looked back
at her.

'Dance with me, Cara?' She turned to see
Robert Hathaway at her side.

'Thank you, no, Robert.' She smiled. 'I'm only a
novice, and besides I really must go rescue Mrs
Varga.'

Robert nodded in understanding and gave her a
rather foolish grin. He was a little drunk, a little
unsteady on his feet, but his eyes focused clearly
on her, and she could see genuine sympathy in
them.

'Don't let that bother you in the slightest,' he
said in a low voice, gesturing with his drink after
the retreating couple. 'There's nothing in it at all.'

Cara followed his gaze across the room to where
Moira and Nicholas were · dancing together,
plastered closely up against each other. She turned
back to Robert.

'Oh, it doesn't bother me,' she said.

Robert cocked his head to one side and gave her
a dry look. 'Of course not. I can see it doesn't.' He
moved a step closer and bent his head down,
speaking in a low, confidential tone. 'Nicholas
could have had Moira years ago if he'd wanted

her. She's just not his type. To my knowledge
there's never been anything between them.'

She raised a hand to stop him. 'Really, Robert,'
she said quickly. 'I don't want to hear . . .'

But Robert had warmed to his subject. 'No,
Cara, you've got to understand. I've known Nick
for a long time. He's not an easy guy to get close
to.' He grinned and waved a wobbly hand in the
air. 'You know how he is, so self-contained and
aloof.' He took a sip of his drink and leaned even
closer. 'But if ever a man was in love with his wife,
it's Nicholas Curzon.' He nodded solemnly, as if
to validate his pronouncement.

Instead of reassuring her, as he intended, his
words only filled her with embarrassment, and
she was grateful when Diana appeared just then at
her husband's side. She narrowed her eyes at him
and deftly lifted the drink out of his hand.

'Come on, Hathaway,' she said drily, gripping
her husband by the arm. 'It's coffee time.' She
lifted her shoulders in a shrug and glanced at
Cara. 'He's harmless,' she said, 'but he talks too
much when he drinks.' She led him away through
the dancers to the bar, where a coffee urn and mugs
had been set up earlier.

Cara started to make her way towards the door
to the hall. She felt suddenly suffocated in the
crowded noisy room, out of her depth, in a strange
world where she didn't know how to handle
herself. At the door she heard the sound of glass
breaking and turned around to see what had
happened.

One of the guests had overturned a drink on the
floor and was now kneeling down to mop it up. It
was nothing serious, and everything seemed to be

under control, but as her glance swept the room, it
fell on Nicholas and Moira. They were standing
under the kissing ring, locked in a tight embrace,
their mouths glued together in a long, clinging
kiss.

Cara stared, hypnotised at the sight. A slow
flush began to rise up in her and spread over her
neck and face. She clenched her fists at her sides,
watching and holding her breath. Moira's back
was towards her, her arms raised around
Nicholas's neck, while his hands were splayed out
flat, one on her bare back, the other just at the
curve of her hips. When at last he raised his head,
Cara found herself looking directly into his eyes.

His gaze was inscrutable. Not by a flicker of
emotion did he reveal what he was thinking or
feeling, but Cara sensed that the question was still
there. She still didn't know how to answer it or
what he expected her to do. She tore her eyes from
his, turned around and walked slowly through the
living and dining rooms to the kitchen.

Lying in bed that night after all the guests had
gone home, staring open-eyed at the ceiling of her
room, Cara tried to sort through the confusion of
her thoughts.

The first and most important step was to try to
understand her own feelings. She knew she had to
be ruthlessly honest with herself, and as she
pondered the events of the evening, two thoughts
became inescapably clear to her.

The first was that she had genuinely enjoyed
dancing in Nicholas's arms, more, she had even
felt strongly attracted to him. All her old
resentments and hatred had vanished into thin air.

She couldn't even remember them or summon up a remote semblance of her old animosity and revulsion at his touch.

The second was that her reaction to seeing Moira Faraday in his arms, kissing him, his kissing her back, had been unmistakably one of blind, unreasoning jealousy. All she could think of was that it was *her* husband Moira was pawing.

Cara knew that she had to resist the temptation to blame Moira or condemn Nicholas for the blatant display on the dance floor. To give in to that anger, to allow herself to become irrational and possessive, would solve nothing. If there was a solution to the chaotic turmoil in her mind, it had to be within herself and not in pointing accusing fingers at them.

She had to think, she kept telling herself as she tossed and turned in her bed, and in order to do so she must refuse to give in to the turbulent emotions that assailed her.

As she grew calmer at last, it came to her with a blinding flash of revelation that she had clearly fallen totally and helplessly in love with Nicholas Curzon. At first she tried to tell herself it was a purely physical reaction to his powerful masculinity and his closeness on the dance floor. She'd had a few glasses of wine, she'd been exhausted from working all day on the party and so unsure of her abilities as a hostess that she was emotionally drained with nervous anticipation.

Then she remembered his past kindnesses to her, his strength that was always at her disposal, supporting her, encouraging her. She thought of the day she'd gone to his office, when she'd looked and felt so shabby in her old clothes, yet still he'd introduced her around proudly to his co-workers. She smiled to herself in the dark as she recalled how firmly he'd handled the saleswoman in the dress shop when she'd called him to check on her claim to be his wife.

There were so many things. His quiet approval of her work at the day-centre, his refusal to dance with anyone else when she wouldn't dance with him herself, the fact that he was providing medical and household care for her mother.

She groaned aloud. What a fool I've been, she thought. Was it too late? Once again she saw in her mind's eye his hands on Moira's body. Were they lovers? Had they ever been lovers? She thought of Robert Hathaway's firm conviction that Nicholas cared only for his wife, for Cara herself. But he'd been half-drunk at the time, and Nicholas had never once said he loved her.

She longed to do something, and even half-rose out of her bed to go to him, tonight, right now, drawn almost irresistibly, and offer herself to him fully as his wife, tell him she loved him, beg his forgiveness for her blind stubborn rejection.

But she knew it wasn't in her to do that, and she fell back dejectedly on the pillows. She was too shy. She had no seductive wiles, she wouldn't even know where to begin, how to approach him. There had to be a way though, she told herself firmly, and as she prayed she would find it, she drifted off to sleep at last.

CHAPTER EIGHT

FROM that night on, there was a subtle change in their relationship that Cara couldn't quite put her finger on, but which she found profoundly disturbing as time went by.

The day after the party, she had awakened with the firm conviction that she would tell him about the dramatic change in her feelings for him. She practised speeches, and at one point, late in the afternoon, she even screwed up her courage to knock at his study door, where he had sequestered himself all day.

'Come in,' he had called out in a curt tone.

She opened the door and stepped inside, all primed to broach the subject. He was sitting at his desk, which was littered with papers and ledger books. He had on a pair of tan chinos, and wore a checked shirt under a dark brown sweater. He looked a little tired, but devastatingly virile and handsome to her. He turned to her, a little impatiently.

'Yes. What is it?' he said shortly.

He stared coldly at her. Cara's heart sank and her nerve failed her. She lowered her eyes and cleared her throat.

'I was just wondering about dinner,' she stammered.

'Yes. What about it?'

He started tapping a pencil on the top of the desk. She must be interrupting something very

148

important, she thought, for him to treat her so abruptly. He obviously wanted to be left alone. She backed away towards the door. Now was not the right time to approach him about personal matters.

She raised her eyes. 'Will you want it at the usual time this evening?'

His lip curled and he looked at her as though she were simple-minded. 'Naturally,' he drawled. 'What on earth made you think I wouldn't?'

Her face reddened as he continued to stare at her. Contempt was written all over his face. 'I'm sorry I disturbed you,' she said stiffly. She whirled round and went back out into the hall, shutting the door quietly behind her. She leaned back against it and closed her eyes. It was hopeless. He acted as though he hated her.

As the days passed and Christmas approached, he seemed to become more and more remote and withdrawn. Cara simply couldn't understand it. Over and over again she searched her mind, trying to think of what could have happened to change his attitude towards her so dramatically.

Granted, before the party they had merely treated each other politely, as rather formal acquaintances, but Cara had grown to appreciate his patience with her and to believe that he was even waiting for her to learn to respond to him as a man rather than an enemy. Each day she had warmed to him more, felt more at ease with him, until finally, during that one fateful dance, she became suddenly aware of how attracted to him she really was.

Now they lived like hostile strangers, and she simply didn't know why. He rebuffed all her

attempts to break through that icy reserve of his
Something had happened at the party to chang
him from the kind, gentle, patient wooer he ha
been to a cold, rejecting alien presence.

He had also started spending most of his night
at the apartment in town. She hardly ever sav
him, and on the rare nights he did drive up to th
lake, they ate dinner in virtual silence. Later, h
would shut himself up in his study for the rest o
the evening and be gone when she got up in th
morning. He was also drinking much more tha
usual, and this only seemed to add to his moros
silence whenever they were together.

Finally, through the process of elimination an
viewing all the evidence as dispassionately a
possible, she came up with the only solution tha
made any sense. Since the change in him was s
marked from the night of the party, it had to b
something that happened that night. He had beel
tender, even loving, until he'd danced with Moira
She remembered the look he had given her whel
she backed off, leaving him with the clingin
blonde, refusing to fight for him, and later th
obvious pleasure he derived from dancing witl
Moira and kissing her under the mistletoe. Add to
that his nocturnal absences ever since, and it wa
clear enough what had happened.

Nicholas was a man of iron will and stron
determination. She thought of how he had insistec
on his right to virtually kidnap her from he
parents' home and later, how he had held hi
desires in check when he realised she couldn'
respond to him physically.

He had given up on her at last. It was the onl
answer. Seeing she wouldn't compete with Moira

or him, sick of waiting for her to come to him, he
ad probably embarked on an affair with Moira
y now. And there was nothing she could do
bout it.

Finally, it was the day before Christmas. They
vere to spend Christmas Eve at the Hathaways',
vhere all of Nicholas's friends traditionally
gathered. Although her heart wasn't in it, Cara
decided it might make her feel better to buy a new
dress for the occasion. She couldn't wear that
dreadful blue velveteen again, and the only other
halfway formal outfit she owned was the black
wedding dress, and she could hardly bear to look
at it hanging in her closet, it brought back so
many painful memories.

She drove into Reno early that morning. There
had been an unexpected warm spell during the last
few days, but snow was predicted by evening, and
she wanted to get to town and back up to the lake
again before it started.

Although she could see a heavy bank of dark
clouds in the far distance to the north, the sun was
shining and sparkling brilliantly overhead on the
snow-covered mountains right now. The tall
evergreens, almost black against the white blanket,
sprang up like silent sentinels. The road was dry,
and it was all so beautiful that Cara felt her spirits
rise considerably as she drove down the now-
familiar road towards Reno.

When she got to town, she parked the car in a
lot and made her way to the first store she had
ever shopped in. Ever since her initial unpleasant
experience there, whenever she'd gone in, the
haughty blonde, humbled by Nicholas, had
greeted her by name and given her service fit for a

queen. Cara had come to quite like her, in fact
and to depend on her judgment.

When she got to the shop, she stopped outside for
a moment to glance at the window displays, where
four mannequins were dressed in glamorous holiday
gowns, all of which were clinging and low-cut. She
thought ruefully of Nicholas's undisguised interest
in Moira's cleavage the night of the party, and her
heart sank. She couldn't compete with that.

It wasn't until she had opened the door to the
shop, however, that the idea hit her. At first, she
was staggered by it and rejected it immediately as
impossible, totally out of character, even a little
sinful, but as it took hold in her mind, she liked it
better and better.

I'll just have to seduce my husband, she decided,
and she marched purposefully inside. If Moira can
get away with it, so can I. Once she made up her
mind, the black depression that had gripped her
for the past two weeks seemed to vanish
miraculously.

Shirley, the blonde saleswoman, appeared from
the back of the shop. When she recognised Cara,
her pale eyes lit up and she came forward to greet
her effusively.

'Oh, Mrs Curzon,' she burbled. 'How nice to see
you! I didn't think you'd be back so soon. How
did the little blue velveteen work out?'

Cara made a face. 'Not very well, Shirley.'
They'd come very close to an argument over
Cara's choice, especially the too-large size. 'You
were right.'

Shirley smiled with satisfaction and shook her
head slowly from side to side as though
admonishing a recalcitrant child. 'I just knew that

dress wasn't right for you, Mrs Curzon. With your figure and lovely colouring you can wear almost anything, but—sorry, dear—that little blue number looked like a sack on you.'

Cara spread her hands wide and sighed. 'All right, all right, I admit it. I was wrong. Now can you find something that might be right for me?'

Shirley raised her finely plucked eyebrows and grinned from ear to ear. 'Really? Do you mean it? Good. You leave it to me. In fact, I think I've got just the thing for you.' She started towards the back storeroom. 'It just came in yesterday in a late holiday shipment, and honestly, I'm not kidding, when I saw it I said to myself, "Wouldn't that be perfect for Mrs Curzon?"'

She disappeared behind the curtain, calling out over her shoulder for Cara to step into a dressing room and start taking off her street clothes.

When Shirley came back, she was carrying several dresses over her arm. She hung them on the metal hook inside the dressing room door, and started unfastening them while Cara finished undressing. They spent the next half hour trying each of them in turn.

By the time they got to the bottom of the pile, Cara was convinced she could never go through with it. Each dress she tried on seemed a little more revealing than the last. She stood in front of the mirror now gazing at her reflection with troubled eyes. This latest creation was a lime green jersey with a halter neck that gaped open and dipped so low in front she would be afraid to breathe in it.

She shook her head sadly. 'No, Shirley. This is impossible. I look like a tart.'

'Honestly, Mrs Curzon, they've all looked marvellous on you. You're just not used to the style.' She helped Cara off with the green dress and hung it on its hanger. Then she fumbled through the crush of dresses down to the bottom again. 'Try this one on again,' she said, holding it up. 'The first one, the one I thought was so right for you.'

Cara stood there in her slip and gazed dubiously at the dress. It was a lovely gown, of a rich clear emerald shade that exactly matched her eyes. The material was a thin, rather stiff silk tissue faille, and the cut of the dress was simplicity itself. It had tiny cap sleeves that barely covered her shoulders, a very wide, very low-cut square neckline that displayed all of her upper chest, barely covered her breasts, and clearly revealed the deep shadowy separation between them.

Cara sighed and allowed Shirley to help her on with it once again. When she looked in the mirror, she shuddered at the image she projected. It was so suggestive. The dress was obviously expensive and in excellent taste. But it certainly left little to the imagination and virtually screamed her availability.

Well, she thought, isn't that what I wanted? She bent over and was so appalled at what she saw that she immediately straightened up. She looked again, still debating. At least it would give Moira a run for her money, and it would pop Nicholas's eyes right out of his head, if only because he'd never in this world expect her to show up wearing such a sexy dress.

She gritted her teeth. 'All right, Shirley. You win. I'll take it.'

Shirley was ecstatic, and the minute Cara stepped out of the dress, she snatched it out of her hands and ran outside to wrap it, as though afraid she would change her mind. When Cara was dressed in her street clothes again, she went over to the counter to sign the charge slip. Shirley handed the package to her with a flourish.

'What you need is a pair of strappy gold sandals with *very* high heels to wear with it,' she advised. 'Mr Curzon is so tall you can get away with it.'

Cara had to agree with her. Before going back to the lot to pick up her car to drive back, she went into a shoe store down the street, and in a short time she found exactly the pair of sandals Shirley had in mind. In fact, when she left, she had to restrain the impulse to go back to show them to her to get her approval. Laughing at herself all the way, she drove directly back to the lake and was home before the first snowflakes began to fall.

Nicholas arrived home quite late that evening because of the snowfall. Cara believed he probably wouldn't have come home at all, even though it was Christmas Eve, if it hadn't been for the party at the Hathaways'. He wouldn't want to miss that.

She was in her room getting ready when she heard his car out in front. It was after eight, and they were due at the Hathaways' at nine. He'd have to hurry to be ready in time.

Mrs Varga had left for her own quarters late that afternoon, and the house was so quiet that Cara could hear every move Nicholas made after he came in and closed the front door behind him. She recognised all the familiar sounds and knew that now he was hanging up his overcoat in the hall cupboard. Then she heard his footsteps crossing over into the living room.

He stayed there long enough for her to realise that he was having his usual quick drink, quite a stiff one these days, and scanning through the evening paper. A little while later, she heard him coming down the hallway to his bedroom and the clinking sound of ice cubes in a glass told her he had mixed himself a second drink, possibly a third.

Then the door to his room opened with a slight familiar creak, and in a few minutes she heard the shower in his bathroom go on. She sat at her dressing table listening to the rush of water, her eyes shut tight, her hands clasped nervously in front of her, imagining him as he undressed to bathe.

She opened her eyes and gazed at her reflection in the mirror. She had taken great pains with her appearance, more than she ever had before in her life. After soaking for half an hour in a warm bath tub scented with bath oil, she had put on a robe and began experimenting with different hairstyles. There wasn't a lot she could do with her long heavy mass of black hair, but she found eventually that if she looped it a little lower over her ears and heightened the chignon more to the top of her head, it looked far more formal and quite flattering to her wide jaw and high cheekbones.

Then came the make-up. She had picked up several new items to try, and was finally satisfied with the effect, after several abortive efforts that had to be creamed and washed off. She'd used just a little eye make-up, mascara and a pale green shadow, and a slightly darker shade of lipstick than she normally wore. She realised she was no

expert at the job, having so little experience, but
when she was through she felt what she had used
suited her.

Last of all, she had put on the dress, zipping it
up the back, and slipped on the new sandals. When
she went to the full-length mirror inside the
bathroom door, she stood there, stunned, for
several seconds. She couldn't believe what she saw.
If the nuns could only see me now, she thought a
little wildly. She looked much taller, of course, in
the very high heels, and her hair and make-up
transformed her face into a far more glamorous
image than she would have thought possible. But
it was the dress that made all the difference.

Her first reaction had been that she couldn't
possibly appear in public looking the way she did.
The little cap sleeves felt very insecure. She'd have
to be very careful how she moved. Of course, the
way the dress was cut, it was out of the question to
wear a slip or a bra underneath it, and she cringed
when she saw that the square neckline actually
dipped down so low in front that it barely covered
the peaks of her breasts. The feel of the silky
material on her bare skin gave her an unsettling,
slightly wicked feeling that was none the less quite
pleasant.

She had agonised over it for several long
minutes, half-tempted to take it off, half-convinced
she should leave it on. Finally, she decided she had
to go through with it. It seemed to be her only
chance to really get Nicholas's attention and break
the awful impasse of the weeks since her wedding.

Sitting there at her dressing table now, all ready
to go, and listening to the sound of Nicholas's
shower running, she still had to make a painful

effort of will to keep from changing her mind again. Granted, the woman in the mirror didn't look at all like Cara O'Neal, but even she had to admit the change was a decided improvement.

Then she heard the shower go off. There was silence for a few minutes, then the hum of an electric razor. Nicholas always shaved closely with a straight-edge in the morning, and only used the electric razor if he was going out in the evening. There was more silence then, and Cara thought she would go mad if she had to sit there for one more minute.

She stood up, wobbling a little on the unfamiliar high heels, and reached out a hand to steady herself on the bedpost. What I need is a drink, she thought. She dreaded facing Nicholas in her new clothes, but at the same time was longing to get it over with, and the suspense was almost more than she could bear. A glass of sherry might quieten her nerves.

She walked warily out into the hall. Nicholas's door was open, and the steamy fragrant aftermath of his recent shower still hung on the air. Although she could hear him pottering in the adjoining bathroom, she couldn't quite see far enough inside to determine whether or not that door was open, too.

Then she heard the telltale clink of ice cubes again and his footsteps. She couldn't see him, but she knew that in just a few seconds he would come into view and would catch her standing there like some gawky adolescent schoolgirl. She turned quickly and had just taken her first step to scurry off down the hall, when the heel of her right shoe gave way and she felt herself falling.

She gave an involuntary cry and braced her
hand against the wall to break her fall. Then, to
her utter dismay, she heard hurried footsteps and
Nicholas's voice coming from behind her.

'Cara? What is it? Are you all right?'

Straightening up, she turned to face him. He
was standing in the doorway of his room, not six
feet from her, a look of concern on his face. There
was a drink in one hand and the other was
stretched out towards her, as though offering her
help. His hair was uncombed, still slightly damp,
and a white towel hung loosely around his neck.
He was wearing the dark trousers of a formal suit,
with an unbuckled leather belt hanging loose inside
the loops. His broad, smooth chest was bare, and
without the support of the belt, his trousers hung
low on his slim hips, revealing the soft mat of dark
hair that started to taper down just below his flat
stomach.

They stared at each other as though paralysed
for several seconds. Then his eyes widened as they
flicked over her slowly from head to toe. She felt
as though she was on fire under that long,
appraising glance.

'I'm sorry,' she stammered. 'I almost fell. I'm all
right now. I'll just go on to the living room and wait
for you there.'

She started to turn, more slowly and carefully
this time, but before she could move away an inch,
his voice cut through the silence like a whip.

'You're not going to the Hathaways' dressed
like that.' His tone was flat and hard, but there
was just enough slur in it to tell her he'd had quite
a bit to drink.

She stared at him. 'Why not?'

His expression was grim. 'Just go change,' he said in a dead even tone.

Her heart sank. Her little ruse had failed. He seemed to be actually repelled by her appearance, and she wondered now how she could ever have imagined she would be able to compete with the glamorous Moira. Full of misery and disappointment, she turned to her own bedroom door. Then she lifted her chin and gazed at him.

'Certainly, Nicholas, if you don't like it.'

His dark eyes held her, and she drew in her breath sharply at the look she saw there; a burning, haunted look that frightened her and held her captive at the same time. He took a step towards her.

'Oh, I like it all right.' There was a rough ferocity in his voice, and she shrank back from him a little. 'I like it too well. And so will every other man there.'

He stopped then, just a few feet away from her, and without lowering his burning gaze, finished off his drink and let the glass fall from his hand.

She looked at him wide-eyed. 'I'm sorry,' she said. 'I thought you wanted me to dress this way. I'll go change.'

Once again, she began to inch her way towards the door, but he wasn't through. 'Why, Cara? Why did you buy it?'

By now she was on the verge of tears. She bit her lower lip and looked up at him through the thick curtain of her dark eyelashes.

'I wanted to please you, Nicholas.' Then, a little more boldly, she said, 'I saw the way you looked at Moira the night of the party. I thought you'd like it if I dressed the way she does.'

'Well, you were wrong,' he bit out in a vicious
one. His forehead creased in a puzzled frown.
Why did you want to please me, Cara?' he asked
a a softer voice. He moved a little closer to her.

'Because . . .' she faltered. 'Because you're my
usband.'

They were almost touching now, standing there
a silence. He stared down into her eyes as though
o probe the secrets of her heart there. Cara felt
erribly warm, Her heart was pounding so hard
nat she swayed a little on her high heels. The
lectricity that sparked between them was almost
alpable.

'Yes,' he said at last. 'I am.' He put a hand on
er bare shoulder, and Cara almost fainted at his
ouch. 'I want to kiss you, Cara,' he whispered.

'Yes,' she breathed, and sank towards him.

Slowly, he lowered his head. She closed her eyes
t the first touch of his lips. They moved gently
ver her mouth at first, sipping at it with a
eathery touch. As he continued to kiss her this
ay, the hand on her shoulder moved languidly
cross her collar bone to clasp her neck, and his
ther arm came around her waist, pulling her
ghtly up against his strong thighs.

She moaned a little deep in her throat as the
and at her neck moved slowly downward, and
hen it began to brush lightly back and forth over
er breasts, an intense wave of pleasure consumed
er and her blood raced like wildfire through her
eins. He was breathing harder now, and his
aouth opened to engulf hers in a hot, moist kiss.
he could taste the whisky he had been drinking,
nd smell the clean fragrance of his breath, his
kin, his damp hair.

Then she felt his tongue forcing her lips apart
and the hand at her breast tightened to knead and
mould first one aroused peak, then the other. She
opened her mouth and allowed his tongue to move
inside it, seeking and probing, and at the same
time, his hand slipped inside the low bodice of her
dress, easing a tiny sleeve down over her shoulder
to free one breast.

The palm of his hand rasped gently against the
taut nipple, then closed around the whole of the
soft mound in a possessive, clutching gesture. His
other hand was on her hips now, pressing her up
against his lower body, grinding her into his male
arousal.

She reached out her hands and put them flat
against his bare chest. As she stroked downward
towards his loose waistband, he stiffened. For a
split second, the hand on her breast stilled and his
mouth became immobile, almost as though a
shock of electricity had just coursed through him,
leaving him momentarily paralysed.

Then he simply lost control. Later, she
wondered if it was because of the strong drinks
he'd consumed so quickly, one right after the
other, but at the time she was so stunned at the
sudden change in him that she couldn't think at
all.

She heard a low growl deep in his throat. He
pushed her a few inches away from him, then
raised both hands to clutch at the neckline of her
dress. In one swift, powerful movement, he ripped
the green dress down over her body until she heard
the seams splitting and it pulled away in his hand.

She stared at him unbelievingly with wide,
horrified eyes, and was shocked at the expression

n his dark face. The eyes were mere slits, the
mouth set in a grim determined line. He was
breathing roughly, in great panting gasps, and
when he reached out blindly for her again, she
shrank back, terrified out of her wits.

'Nicholas!' she cried. 'Stop! Please stop! What
are you doing?'

He merely snarled at her and swooped her up in
his powerful arms. He kicked the door of her
bedroom open, strode to the edge of her bed, and
dropped her unceremoniously down on top of it.

He stood there in the shadows cast by the light
spilling in from the hall, glaring down at her, his
fists planted on his hips, his legs apart. She
cowered back against the pillows, vainly trying to
cover herself with her hands, too frightened to
move. She'd never get away from him anyway. He
was too strong and too fast for her.

His chest was heaving, his black hair in total
disarray. He reached down and tore off the flimsy
silk underpants, her only remaining garment, and
threw them on the floor. She watched him,
terrified, as he unzipped his trousers and slid them
down to the floor at his feet until he stood there
naked and fully aroused before her.

'You wanted to please me, did you, Cara?' he
snarled at her in a low, menacing voice. 'You've
tormented me for months, gagging with nausea
whenever I came near you, showing me with every
word, every gesture, how much you loathed my
touch.' He put his hands flat on the bed and
leaned over her, fixing her with a look of cold
contempt. 'And now you have the gall to taunt me
by running around half-naked in that provocative
dress.'

'Nicholas!' she begged. 'Please listen to me.' Her teeth were chattering and tears began to spill from the corners of her eyes. 'I never meant . . .'

'Be quiet!' he roared. 'I don't want to hear any more of your excuses. You seduced me this time, lady, and your delicate sensibilities aren't going to stop me now.' He grinned wickedly and put a knee on the bed. 'But you're right about one thing. I am your husband. I *won* you, Cara, and tonight the winner will take all.'

CHAPTER NINE

WHEN Cara awoke the next morning, she was alone in the bed. She couldn't recall Nicholas leaving and wondered if she could have fainted at some point. She raised her head up from the pillow and groaned aloud. Every muscle and every inch of her skin on her naked body was sore and tender.

As memory flooded back and she began to recall the painful details of the previous night, she couldn't stop the tears that stung her eyes and rolled down her cheeks on to her pillow. She tried to block hideous memories out of her mind, but they kept crowding in on her, filling her mind with despair.

She felt so humiliated, so violated. Nicholas had been like a wild animal, throwing himself on to her without a word or any attempt at lovemaking, taking her roughly, uncaring of the pain of that first deep thrust into her inexperienced body, again and again and again. She'd never forgive him, never in her life.

She wiped the tears away and shifted her aching body gingerly until she was in a sitting position. All she wanted now was to get out of this house, away from Nevada, away from that madman she'd married and back to the shelter of her own home at the ocean. She'd known from the beginning that he was dangerous, perhaps even a criminal, but had been lulled into a false sense of security by his pretence of kindness and understanding.

Wincing at the soreness between her legs, she eased herself out of bed and tiptoed cautiously to the door. She pressed her ear up against it, listening, straining to catch any sounds of his presence, but all she could hear was the sound of Mrs Varga's radio playing in the kitchen.

She snapped the lock shut and leaned her forehead against the door with a sigh. She would be safe now. She went into the bathroom and drew a bath of warm water, sprinkling it liberally with soothing bath oil. She got in before it was full, and lay there blissfully soaking until her limbs and skin began to feel more normal.

As she dried off, dressed and pinned up her hair, she wondered how she was going to get away. She dreaded facing him. Could she stay in her room until tomorrow, pretend she was sick, and leave when he'd gone down to his office in Reno? She walked over to the window, pulled the heavy curtain aside and blinked as the fresh white snowfall blinded her momentarily.

Christmas Day, she thought sadly. She would like to go to church. Maybe that would help. Later she'd call her family. Tomorrow she would leave. The roads would be clear by then. She would drive to the airport and leave the car there. As she made her plans, she began to feel much better, even, she realised, a little hungry.

She decided to venture out of her room after all. She'd have to if she wanted to get to Mass and use the telephone. What could he do to her if she did see him? Mrs Varga was in the house. She wouldn't tell him she was leaving tomorrow. She wouldn't speak to him at all.

She lifted her chin, squared her shoulders and

marched to the door. Unlocking it, she walked out into the hall, then down to the kitchen. Mrs Varga was alone, humming along with the Christmas carols coming from the radio and rolling out pastry dough.

'Merry Christmas, Mrs Varga,' Cara called to her from the doorway.

Mrs Varga looked up and smiled. 'Oh, and the same to you, Mrs Curzon. I hope you're feeling better. Such a shame to be sick on Christmas Eve and miss the Hathaways' party.' She attacked the pie crust again, still rambling on. 'When Mr Curzon told me about it before he left this morning, I just felt so bad for you.'

Cara took a hesitant step into the kitchen. 'He's—ah—he's already gone, then?' she asked in an uncertain tone.

'Oh, my, yes. Isn't it too bad he had to leave you alone on Christmas Day? Business!' she snorted. 'You'd think they'd let the poor man at least enjoy the holidays.'

She gave Cara a commiserating look. Cara smiled weakly. 'Yes, you would,' she agreed. She went to the refrigerator to get a glass of orange juice and poured herself a cup of coffee at the stove.

'I'll put your toast on in just a minute here,' Mrs Varga said, panting a little from her exertions with the rolling pin. 'Oh, I almost forgot. Mr Curzon left a note for you. He put it with your package from him under the tree.'

'Oh,' Cara said weakly. A note. Then a quick surge of anger spread through her. He could keep his note! She wanted nothing from him. Thank God, he was gone and she wouldn't have to endure his hateful presence. She turned to Mrs Varga. 'Did he say how long he'd be gone?'

'He said at least a week. He put it all in the note.'

A week! Waves of relief washed over her. There was plenty of time.

Since Mrs Varga had gone to midnight Mass the night before, Cara drove to the little chapel on the other side of the lake by herself after breakfast. She was just as glad to be alone. She was fond of the voluble housekeeper, but on this particular morning, she wasn't in the mood to hear any more praise of Nicholas Curzon.

It was a beautiful day. The small storm that had blanketed the area with snow yesterday afternoon had passed over, and the sky was a glittering metallic blue. The roads had been cleared and sanded early that morning so that she had no trouble driving on them.

By the time Mass was over, she had almost forgotten Nicholas's savage attack on her. It was already beginning to fade, like a terrible nightmare that had no reality or power to harm her in the light of day. In fact, driving home over the familiar road and drinking in the fresh clean air, she realised that in spite of her gruesome experience, she actually felt better than she had in weeks.

There would be no more playing games with that dreadful man or trying to outguess him, no more homesickness for the ocean, no more worry about competing with Moira, and no more having to endure his demanding lust. With the decision to leave for good firmly resolved, she felt calm and confident.

He didn't want her any more, anyway. He'd made that clear ever since the party. Last night had merely been a form of punishment for her past rejection of him. He'd used her body as he would a prostitute's, worse, without the slightest concern for her pleasure or feelings, merely as a form of revenge.

In fact, she decided, as she pulled into the driveway of the house, he'd probably be glad to be rid of her. She wondered for the hundredth time why he had been so insistent on blackmailing her into marriage in the first place. Was it only because an unattainable woman was a challenge to his male vanity? Since she'd been living with him she'd seen how attractive other women found him. They all seemed to think she'd won some kind of prize in marrying him.

If they only knew what a beast he really was, she snorted to herself as she let herself into the house. It was very quiet inside. Mrs Varga had most of the day off, of course, and not even the sound of her radio was there to break the stillness.

It was after twelve, and Cara felt hungry after her meagre breakfast. She decided to fix herself a sandwich from the turkey Mrs Varga had roasted yesterday. Then, after lunch, she would pack her things, and call her mother later to tell her she was coming home.

As she passed through the living room on her way to the kitchen, she glanced at the small Christmas tree she and Mrs Varga had set up and decorated two nights ago. Nicholas had been gone, as usual, spending the night at the apartment in town, and hadn't seemed to be at all interested in anyway. It looked rather forlorn sitting there on

a red-draped table in front of the window. M
Varga had turned on the tiny, blinking colour
lights, probably in an effort to strike a chee
holiday note, but with the mu. n brighter s
shining in on it, the effect was lost.

Before she turned away from the dreary sight
the pathetic little tree, her eye was caught by a 1
oblong package underneath it, the only one the
She hadn't known what to get Nicholas. Th
relations had been so strained recently, and
seemed to have so little interest in anything to
with Christmas, that she just hadn't bought hin
gift at all. Except for the now ruined emer:
dress, she thought bitterly, which had really be
bought for his benefit.

She was surprised, then, that he had 1
something for her, and she couldn't help being
little curious. She took a step closer to the tr
The package wasn't wrapped. It was a plain wh
cardboard box with only a red ribbon ti
awkwardly around it. Tucked underneath 1
ribbon was a square envelope of heavy, crea
coloured paper. On it, in Nicholas's bold har
was written simply, 'Cara', in slashing bla
letters.

For one moment only she hesitated, sor
tempted to read the note, open the package. Th
she called to mind again his cruelty and h
brutally he had treated her last night, and s
made herself turn away. I want it to be there wh
he comes back and finds me gone, she thou;
savagely. I want him to know that I hate him
much I wouldn't even stoop to read his note
open his present.

After lunch, she went into her room to pa

She had decided she would take nothing with her except what she had come with. She wanted nothing that would remind her ever again of her life here. She'd have to use a little of his money for her plane ticket to Seattle and the bus to Southport, but she'd had a few hundred dollars of her own when she arrived anyway, so they'd be even.

She took out her suitcase from the back of the wardrobe and set it on the bed. She filled it first with her old underwear, a pair of shabby denim jeans and a few sweaters. She took off the new red suit she'd worn to church and hung it up in the wardrobe alongside her other recent purchases, then dressed in her old grey skirt, white shirt and green sweater. She'd wear her black dress and old coat on the plane, a fitting colour for the death of her marriage.

When she was through sorting clothes, she pushed all the new outfits far back in the wardrobe. She didn't even want to be tempted to take any of them with her. She'd burn the ripped green dress that was still lying on the floor where Nicholas had thrown it last night. It was beyond repair.

At the back of the wardrobe, high up on the shelf, her gaze fell on the box that Nicholas had given her on their wedding night. Just the thought of that lovely white gown made her so angry that she had to repress the impulse to pull it down and burn it, too. Or better, cut it to shreds and leave it on the bed for him to find when he came home, her parting gift to him.

In the end, she knew she couldn't do it. The habit of thrift was too strong in her from all the

years of near-poverty. It was a beautiful gown.
Maybe, she thought wryly, he could give it to
Moira.

Finished at last, she decided it was time to
'phone her mother. In a way, she dreaded it. In all
her calls home, she had consistently assured her
mother that everything was going smoothly in her
new life. She hadn't wanted to worry her or add to
the burden of guilt her father already felt for what
he'd done to her. Now, she'd have to tell them the
truth, or as much of it as was absolutely necessary.
She wouldn't need to go into any of the gory
details.

She went back to the living room to make her
call, and as she dialled the number and listened to
the ringing tone, her eye fell once again on the sad
little tree in the window, the lonely white package
beneath it. She wished now she had used the
telephone in the kitchen, but it was too late.

'Hello,' came her mother's voice.

'Mother!' Cara cried. 'Are you up? Why aren't
you in bed?'

She heard her mother's low chuckle. 'I'm not in
bed because I don't need to be in bed,' she replied
gaily.

It had been years since Cara had heard her
mother sound so strong, so happy, and tears of joy
filled her eyes. She couldn't speak.

'The doctor tells me I'm in a sort of remission,'
her mother went on to explain. 'He doesn't really
understand it, and it won't last, but we just take
one day at a time.'

'Oh, Mother, what wonderful news! It's the best
Christmas present I could hope for.'

'Now don't go getting your hopes up,' her

mother warned sternly. 'I'm not cured. The cancer is too advanced for that. But, apparently it's not going to kill me just yet.' She chuckled again. 'The new doctor Nicholas sent down here from Seattle tells me it's none of his doing, but I'll never believe it. And,' she added fervently, 'I'll never be able to express my gratitude to that husband of yours. The wonderful woman he hired to come in to cook and clean has taken such a load off my mind.'

Cara hadn't a clue what her mother was talking about. She knew vaguely that Nicholas had made arrangements for household and medical help for her mother, but she'd been so preoccupied by her own problems, she never had learned the details. She hadn't even called home for weeks.

'Well, that's wonderful, Mother,' she said weakly at last. How could she tell her now she was leaving this paragon who had so much for her? Well, she decided, she didn't have to, not yet. 'Mother,' she said, 'I'm coming home for a visit. Nicholas is out of town this week on business, and it seemed like an ideal time. I thought I'd get a plane out tomorrow, if it's all right.'

'Oh, darling, tomorrow Patrick is driving me up to Seattle for some more tests. I'll have to stay at the clinic for a few days. Of course, you can come any time you like, but maybe you should wait until I know when I'll be able to go home again.'

Cara's spirits plunged. With both Patrick and her mother gone, there really wasn't much point in leaving so soon. Her father and other brothers would be out working on the boats all day. She should spend a few more days at the child-care centre, too, instead of just suddenly dropping out of sight. She owed it to Diana to find a replacement for her. Nicholas would be gone for a week. There was no hurry. She spoke to her mother again.

'Maybe it would be best to wait, then,' she said. 'Why don't you call me when you get back from Seattle? Or, better yet, call before you leave, and I can ride back to Southport with you and Patrick. I can extend my visit as long as I want.'

Her mother laughed. 'Oh, you'll want to be there when Nicholas gets back, I'm sure. After all, you're still newlyweds.' She paused for a moment, then lowered her voice in a more serious tone. 'Cara, I can't tell you how pleased I am that you're so happy with him. I knew it would work out. That's why I encouraged you to marry him in the first place, even though the circumstances were a little—ah—unusual.'

'You knew it would work out?' Cara repeated weakly. 'How did you know?'

'Oh, a mother's intuition, I guess. He just seemed right for you, and it was crystal clear to me that he was very much in love with you. I knew eventually you'd learn to care for him. He's a fine man.'

Cara couldn't listen for another minute. One more word about how wonderful Nicholas was, and she'd scream.

'I'd better go now, Mother. Give my love to Dad and the boys. I'll see you in a few days.'

After she'd hung up the telephone, Cara sat rigidly in her chair, virtually beside herself with frustration. She wished now with all her heart she'd had the nerve to tell her mother what a vicious brute that 'fine' man really was. How could intelligent people be so wrong about a person?

Since she couldn't go home for a few days, she thought with a sigh, she might as well unpack some of her things. Tomorrow was Friday. The day-care centre would be closed, since it was the day after Christmas, as well as over the weekend. She'd have to wait until Monday to talk to Diana. She would go home Tuesday, she decided. Tuesday, at the latest.

By Sunday, the details of that dreadful night had faded into a dim memory in Cara's mind. She kept busy during the day, taking long walks around the lake, reading in front of the fire, talking to Mrs Varga. At night she slept like a log.

On Christmas night she had taken Nicholas's package and note out from under the tree and hidden them in one of her dressing-table drawers. Now that she had to delay her departure, she didn't want Mrs Varga to see them still lying there unopened. When she left on Tuesday, she would take them out again and place them conspicuously on the mantelpiece over the living-room fireplace so he wouldn't miss seeing them.

Better yet, she could put them in Nicholas's bedroom. Mrs Varga wouldn't be going in there to clean or make his bed until he came back, so she might as well do it today. She went to her room and took the package out of the dressing-table drawer, then crossed the hall to his room and stepped inside the half-open door.

It was as neat as ever, and she could smell the lingering trace of his unique fragrance. She looked around the room for a good place to leave the package, and as she did so, a strange feeling began to steal over her. Oddly disturbed by it, unable to put a name to it, she frowned and took another step inside.

On closer inspection, she found that there were, indeed, little traces of Nicholas here and there in spite of the spotless austerity of the room. An extra set of keys on the dresser, his dark blue bathrobe flung carelessly at the foot of the bed, a pair of well-polished shoes by the wardrobe door.

Drawn by the curious power she still didn't understand, she moved in a sort of trance into the bathroom. His towels were hanging neatly on the racks, and a white terry cloth robe hung on the back of the door. On the tile counter was a half-empty bottle of his aftershave, a tube of toothpaste and the small leather box where he kept his straight-edge razor.

Unthinking, she reached out to touch the robe, and sudden unbidden tears sprang to her eyes. I loved him, she thought. Then she caught a glimpse of her face in the mirror, twisted with grief, and came to her senses.

Love! How could she ever have thought she loved a man like that! Even if she could bring herself to forgive his brutal treatment of her, he was probably off in some hotel with Moira Faraday anyway.

She turned on her heel and started to retrace her steps back through the bedroom. Then she remembered the package, still clutched in her hand. She hesitated, her mind churning with conflicting emotions. Finally, she heaved a long sigh. She had to do it. She simply couldn't leave without knowing what was in that mysterious package and what his final words to her had been, or she'd wonder about it for the rest of her life.

She sank down on the bed. It was late afternoon and growing dark by now, so she switched on a lamp by the side of the bed. She decided to read the note first. She was far more interested in what he had to say than in what he could give her.

She slid the envelope out from under the red ribbon and tore it open. Inside was one large sheet of paper, covered in his bold slashing hand.

'It is Christmas morning,' she read,

'and in a few moments I'll be leaving for Los Angeles on a long-postponed business trip. It seemed an appropriate time to go. I won't be back until next Wednesday night. That should give you ample time to leave, as I'm sure you are determined to do after what has happened.

I just want you to know before you go how deeply and dreadfully sorry I am about the way I forced myself on you last night. I've never done a thing like that in my life, never even been remotely tempted. It was unforgivable. I'd like to blame it on the amount I'd had to drink, but I know that's a poor excuse. Please believe I am as deeply shocked at my behaviour as you must be.

In the box is my Christmas gift to you, one I've planned to give you for some time. Now it will be my parting gift, too. I would have bought you jewels and furs if I'd thought you wanted them, but I know by now that your only wish is to be free of me.

Once again, I'm sorry. For everything. I can see now how wrong I was, right from the beginning, to think I could force your love. And so you *are* free of me, Cara. I won't bother you ever again.'

When she had finished, she read it again. She didn't know what to think. He was letting her go, that much was clear, but it didn't sound as though he wanted her to. And what did he mean by forcing her 'love'? He had never wanted her love. Had he?

Still bewildered, she untied the red ribbon and lifted the lid off the cardboard box. She stared inside. There was no tissue wrapping, nothing but some pieces of paper. Had he given her money, written her a cheque? She picked them up, and as she scanned them, her mouth fell open, and tears stung her eyes.

They were the notes on her father's boats! Examining them more closely, she saw that he had endorsed them over to her. They were now her property, whether she stayed or left. The one hold he had on her, and he was renouncing it, giving it back to her. Finally, the tears spilled over, and she flung herself face down on his bed, sobbing.

As the tension drained out of her along with her tears, different thoughts about him began to crowd into her mind. Her mother's high opinion of him. Mrs Varga's slavish devotion. The respect shown him by his business colleagues. The affection of his friends. The way he had protected her from unpleasantness at the dress shop and attended to her needs at the bank. His kindness and generosity.

As she calmed down and the sobs subsided, her thoughts turned to memories of a different kind. His strongly muscled body chopping wood outdoors that day. His dazzling good looks in the formal dinner jacket. The glimpse she had caught of his desire for her breaking through his quiet reserve from time to time, desire he had kept carefully in check for months, out of consideration for her, desire that had spilled over in a fit of uncontrolled passion only when she had set out deliberately to seduce him. Granted, he had never told her in so many words, but his every action, from the very beginning, shouted that he loved her.

She thought again of that fateful Christmas Eve, this time from a new perspective, recalling the powerful effect his tender lovemaking had had on her before he lost control, how she had responded to him, how good his mouth had felt pressing on hers and his body as she strained against him. What was more, she hadn't felt a trace of the old nausea.

She got up from the bed and went into his bathroom again. At the sink, she washed her face off with cool water, then dried it on one of his towels, breathing in his lingering scent. When she looked in the mirror, she saw a new Cara, bright-eyed, eager and full of hope. She knew now exactly what she had to do, and she wouldn't look back.

CHAPTER TEN

CARA had no idea what time to expect Nichola.
home, so on that Wednesday afternoon she called
the Reno airport and was told that the Los
Angeles flight was due in at eight-fifteen that
night. Give him an hour to collect his baggage and
drive back up to Lake Tahoe, she thought, and
he'd be home by nine at the earliest. She only
hoped he wouldn't decide to stay at the apartment
in town. There hadn't been any new snow, and the
roads were clear. Surely he'd want to unpack and
get his mail?

Mrs Varga left as usual as soon as she had
prepared dinner, a little after six o'clock, and Cara
started making her preparations. She laid out a
fire in the living room, checked to make sure the
drinks' cabinet was stocked with his favourite
Scotch, and wrapped the turkey sandwiches she'd
made for him and put them in the refrigerator.

Then she had her bath, a long relaxing soak to
quiet her jumpy nerves. She was determined to go
through with her plan to the end, come what may,
but she couldn't control her pounding heart and
shaking hands.

After drying herself, she went to the wardrobe
and reached far back in the wardrobe to take
down the box that had lain for so long up on the
shelf. She took out the filmy, delicate white
nightgown, and as she slipped it over her head, her
knees almost gave way. She slumped down heavily

n the chair in front of her dressing table and
egan to brush out her long black hair. Tonight
he would not pin it up.

She decided at the last minute to put on her
obe and slippers. She couldn't quite bring herself
o face him with only the gown on. What if Moira
ad gone with him and he brought her home? She
vent back into the living room to make her final
noves. She had a little trouble getting the fire
,oing, and by the time it took hold and flared up
nto a fine blaze, it was after eight o'clock. She
urned on the stereo set low, choosing a station
hat played only old romantic tunes and switched
ll the lamps off except one dim one in a far
orner. Then she sat down in front of the fire to
vait.

The last time she checked her watch, it had been
ine-thirty, and she began to doubt he was
:oming. She must have dozed off then, because the
lext thing she knew, she was sitting bolt upright
ind listening to the sound of a key in the front
loor lock.

The fire had died down to a few flickering
lames over a bed of glowing coals, but she
:ouldn't make herself move to get up and put on a
'resh log. She leaned her head back on the
:ushions of the couch and closed her eyes tight,
praying for courage. She took a deep breath and
,lowly rose to her feet just as Nicholas appeared in
the doorway, still in his overcoat, his suitcase in
his hand.

They stood there, not ten feet apart, staring at
each other. The look on his face and the sharp
intake of his breath told her he was astonished to
see her, but he covered it quickly and simply

continued to stare. Cara was the first to drop her gaze, and as she did, she saw that the blue bathrobe had come untied and was hanging open to reveal the white nightgown underneath.

Finally he spoke. 'You're still here,' he said.

'Yes.'

He set down his suitcase and walked slowly towards her, peeling off his overcoat and throwing it back on top of it. 'Why, Cara?'

Flustered, she blurted out the first thing that popped into her head. 'Just tell me one thing, Nicholas. Was Moira with you on your trip?'

He gave her a puzzled look. 'Moira? Why on earth would Moira be with me? Of course not.' He kept coming towards her until finally he was standing directly in front of her, looking down at her and frowning. 'Why are you still here, Cara?'

He smelled of the fresh outdoors, and she could feel the cold still on his skin and clothes in the warm room. He looks so tired, she thought. His face was hollow and gaunt, the high cheekbones standing out in prominent relief, the fine lines at the corners of his eyes deeply etched, and a little muscle throbbed at his jawline, and she longed to reach out and smooth it all away.

Instead, she gathered all her courage and looked straight into his hooded dark eyes. 'I'm still here because . . .' She faltered, took a deep breath, and went on. 'Because I love you. Because I want to be your wife—if you still want me.'

His eyes widened in total disbelief. 'If I still want you?' he said hoarsely. 'Cara, I love you more than my life.'

At that, she uttered a little cry and sank towards him. His arms came around her, and she buried her head in his shoulder, trembling with relief and joy. He stroked her long hair gently and lowered his head to murmur softly in her ear.

'I've always loved you, my darling girl, from the first moment I set eyes on you ten years ago when you were only a child.' He put the palms of his hands flat against her cheeks and forced her head up to face him. 'I waited for you to grow up,' he said simply. 'Those yearly trips to Southport were the high points of my life. The fishing was only an excuse. I know now I probably went about it all wrong, forcing you to marry me like that, but when your father told me you wanted to be a nun, I grew desperate. I had to have you, don't you see? I had to.'

He kissed her then, and her lips opened of their own accord to greet him. His arms tightened around her as the kiss deepened, and she pressed herself eagerly against him. His mouth moved to her forehead, her cheeks, her chin, her ear, little passionate kisses that left her breathless.

'Can you ever forgive me, darling, for what happened before I left?' he murmured at her throat.

'I have forgiven you,' she breathed.

'I just went a little crazy,' he said. He raised his head and looked down at her. 'At the party, when we danced, when I kissed you under the mistletoe, and you seemed to be responding to me at last, I got my hopes up. Then when you backed off and gave way to Moira, I was so disappointed that I could hardly bear to even look at you for days afterwards.'

She nodded. 'I wondered why you were so cool to me.' She wrinkled her forehead. 'I didn't understand, Nicholas. I've had no experience i[n] these things. I thought you were tired of waitin[g] for me, that you wanted Moira.'

'My darling Cara, if I'd wanted Moira I coul[d] have had her years ago. There's never bee[n] anything between us, never. I've had my share o[f] amorous adventures over the years, but never wit[h] Moira, and never, in fact, with any woman you'[ll] ever encounter.' He smiled crookedly. 'I've bee[n] very discreet, you see. I was waiting for you.'

She put her hands on his face then and ran he[r] fingers over the faint stubble on his chin, the fin[e] strong jawline. She smoothed out the lines aroun[d] his eyes and felt the hollows of his cheeks, he[r] heart so full of tenderness and love for this ma[n] she thought it would burst.

His eyes burned into her. 'I want you, Cara,' h[e] said in a low voice.

'Yes,' she said. 'Oh, yes, Nicholas. I want you[,] too.'

Slowly, he reached out and pulled the robe of[f] her shoulders until she stood before him in the delicate white gown he had given her. With his eyes still feasting on her, he took off his jacket[,] loosened his tie and started unbuttoning his shirt. Cara stared, entranced, as his bare chest was revealed.

After he had shrugged out of his shirt, he put his hands on her shoulders again and ran them slowly down until they came to rest on her breasts. Gasping with sheer pleasure, she closed her eyes and gave in completely to the delicious sensations aroused in her as his fingers brushed lightly over her nipples.

Then he crushed her to his bare chest, and his

mouth descended on hers in a hot, open-mouthed kiss. His tongue darted inside her mouth and the hands on her breasts kneaded and stroked until she thought she would go mad with the fire that was coursing through her.

They sank slowly to the floor. He knelt before her and pulled the gown over her head, then clasped her so closely in his arms that her naked breasts came up against his bare chest. Slowly, he eased her down on her back in front of the fire and leaned over her, bracing himself with one hand flat on the floor, while the other explored her body eagerly, her breasts, her stomach, her thighs.

'Touch me, Cara,' he whispered.

She smiled and reached up to run her hands through his dark crisp hair until it fell over his forehead. Then she placed her palms on his broad chest, moved them over his tautly muscled arms and shoulders and back. His skin was smooth and hot and slightly damp and quivered under her light touch. When she reached the waistband of his trousers, she gave him a shy, enquiring look. He nodded his encouragement.

She unbuckled his belt then, and slipped her fingers inside the loosened waistband to feel the rough hair that started there on his lower abdomen. With a sharp indrawn gasp, he put his hand over hers and pressed it tight against his body, forcing it lower, until she became fully aware of his intense need of her.

With a groan, he moved away and slid out of his trousers and pants. When he came back to her, he kissed her on the mouth, then lowered his lips to her throat, her breast, and with one hand firmly clasping the full white mound from underneath, he

opened his mouth to cover the throbbing peak
suckling there until Cara began to twist beneath
him, hardly able to endure the sharp stabs of
pleasure that coursed through her whole body. He
moved his lips to her other breast and slid his
hand down over her ribcage, her hips, the inside of
her thighs, until it finally came to rest between
them.

She cried out at the sheer, unexpected thrill of
ecstasy his touch created in her, and at last he
covered her body with his own and she felt his
hard pulsing desire throb against her.

'Oh, please, Nicholas,' she begged. 'Please.
Now.'

Slowly he entered her, and as the passionate
crescendo began to build with each thrust, she felt
herself go weak with the sensations that filled her
entire being, mind, body and soul, until finally she
reached the pinnacle of excruciating tension. She
couldn't stop herself from crying out her joy at
that glorious climax. She felt herself shattering
into a million little pieces, heard her husband's
answering shout of release, and then sank down
into near-oblivion, satisfied at last.

She lay, still panting, in his arms for several long
minutes while he stroked her hair and face
tenderly, telling her of his love in a low, intimate
voice. Finally, she was able to open her eyes. She
looked up at him, full of wonder.

'I never knew, Nicholas,' she said with something
like awe. 'I never knew it would be like that.'

He bent to kiss her lightly on the mouth. 'It isn't
always.' He smiled. 'I think love has a lot to do
with it.'

He put his head on her breast and they both

dozed off in front of the fire. When she stirred awake again, the fire was reduced to low, smouldering coals. She shivered a little. She looked down at her sleeping husband. He had moved slightly away from her in his sleep, but still had one hand placed possessively over her breast. His strong naked body gleamed in the red light of a sudden last spurt of flame from the fireplace. She should wake him soon, she thought, and go to bed. Together, from now on.

She smiled to herself as she thought of telling their grandchildren how he had won her in a poker game. It would make a good story. But this time, she decided a little smugly, it was the loser who took all.

Harlequin Presents

Coming Next Month

Available in August wherever paperback books are sold, or through Harlequin Reader Service:

In the U.S.
P.O. Box 1397
Buffalo, N.Y.
14240-1397

In Canada
P.O. Box 2800, Postal Station A
5170 Yonge Street
Willowdale, Ontario M2N 6J3

Explore love with Harlequin in the Middle Ages, the Renaissance, in the Regency, the Victorian and other eras.

Relive within these books the endless ages of romance, set against authentic historical backgrounds. Two new historical love stories published each month.

Available starting August wherever paperback books are sold.